Back
To
Carolina

Seth Sjostrom

wolfprintMedia, LLC
Hernando Beach, FL

For information, contact wolfprintMedia, LLC.

Second Edition
ISBN-13: 978-1-7349376-3-3

1. Dean Taylor (Fictitious character)-Fiction. 2. Romance-Beach-Fiction. 3. Back to Carolina-Fiction I. Title.

First wolfprintMedia Digital edition 2020. wolfprintMedia is a trademark of wolfprintMedia, LLC.

For information regarding bulk purchases, please contact wolfprintMedia, LLC, at wolfprint@hotmail.com.

United States of America

To my family- Tom, Linda, Steven and Tonya Sjostrom. Memories of playing in alligator-infested lakes and countless days on Carolina beaches.

Kathi Sjostrom, my prize for living and learning along the way.
One of these days I'll grow up. Maybe.

To all of my friends from Southport, NC and amazing relationships forged while attending the University of North Carolina at Wilmington. I learned a lot from you, sorry it took a couple of decades for it to sink in.

Jen Boles, my friendly, encouraging editor who helps my words navigate the pages properly.

Chapter One -
A Pacific Coast Life

Dean Taylor sat at the center of a massive executive boardroom table. Completing the final part of his pitch, he tossed the thick packet of papers in front of him and leaned back in his padded leather, high-back chair.

He studied the expression of each person across the table from him before allowing his gaze to penetrate the bank of windows behind them. The Southern California cityscape gave way to the Pacific skyline. He had perfected this closing technique through dozens of transactions.

Studying the space between the buildings, he knew somewhere, not too far beyond, were the rolling waves crashing into Santa Monica's beaches. These drunken thoughts allowed him to seem unaffected by the whispering his clients shared amongst themselves. For Dean, the ocean allowed him to remove himself from the stress and tension of the high-stakes negotiations.

Dean was ripped from his brief meditation as the corporate attorney for his client cleared his throat and clasped his hands together. His peers sat up straight and reassembled into their spots following their huddle.

"So, we like what we see, the price, however…" the attorney began.

Dean quickly nodded his head in understanding. Without saying anything further, he carefully straightened the papers in front of him; his eyes strictly focused on his task. Sliding out his chair, he stood up, to the bewilderment of his guests and his team. Pivoting away from the table and his clients, Dean made his way towards the door.

"Well," the attorney sputtered abruptly, "Surely, we can work on the fee…"

Dean stopped, tapping his papers against his chest for a moment. He spun back toward his guests, "You, yourself, have stated the value of what we have proposed. We only need one, two at the most partners in your space. If you want to be one, fantastic, we would love that partner to be you. If not, I…."

"Okay, okay, you have a deal, Mr. Taylor."

Dean dropped his rigid stance and visage, offering a broad smile, "Very well, we'll execute the contract, and we will welcome you as one of Dana Holdings' key partners."

Signed contracts in hand, Dean took a victory lap through the office to the cheers of his team and the reigning senior executives of his firm. As the revelry ensued toward the executive suites, Dean's boss called him into his office.

"Nice work. You have certainly proven you can handle yourself. Look, I know you are making good money in your current role. We have begun the search for our next partner—someone younger, who someday in the future, can take the reins. Maintain our legacy. We think that person is you, Dean," Marshall Givings declared.

Dean struggled to harness his exuberant expression, "I am flattered, sir. I love what I do. I'm ready to take whatever next step you feel is appropriate."

"Glad to hear that. We are on the doorstep of a major takeover, and we want you to lead it," Marshall said.

"Great. I am ready to go," Dean said, clapping his hands softly together as he leaned forward. "What company?"

"Cape Fear Commercial."

Dean nodded, "I'm familiar with them. They make special parts for boats."

"Yes, that's Cape Fear. The deal is going to take some work, so you might have to spend some time with them," his boss cautioned.

"Sure, no problem."

"We have arranged an expense account for you, first-class accommodations," Dean's boss shared.

"Perfect. Their San Diego office?"

Marshall laughed, "No, their powers to be are in North

Carolina. Your old stomping grounds, right? Should be perfect for you."

Dean shook his head, stunned, "North Carolina? Are you sure I need to go *there*? I have the team to lead here, plenty of remote resources. Let's invite them out here- set them up in grand California style?"

"I thought about that. But here's the truth, we want Cape Fear more than they need us. Companies from the South are all about relationships. They want to know that if we take them over, we will take care of their people."

The CEO studied Dean, trying to decipher his employee's reaction, "Is this going to be a problem?"

Dean shook himself, "No, sir. I'll have this wrapped up in days."

Laughing, Marshall nodded, "I bet you will. In the meantime, go out of here and celebrate. You deserve it, and Monday is going to come soon enough."

Dean nodded and stood up to leave, trying to stifle a grimace. Outside of his boss's office, he leaned against the wall out of Marshall's view, let out a deep sigh, and shook his head at the opportunity.

Chapter Two –
Leaving Cali

Dean sat atop his surfboard, looking out at the horizon, eyeing the incoming swells.

"So, they're sending you to North Carolina," his friend Ray broke his gaze.

Offering a sullen nod, Dean replied, "Yep."

Ray, having heard many of Dean's exploits from college, snickered, "Should be fun."

Dean grimaced, "Yeah, I'm not so sure. There was a reason I left."

"More like *reasons* from the stories you've told me," Ray laughed. "Many reasons– blonde, brunette, redhead…"

Furrowing his brows, Dean glared, "It wasn't *all* like that. I had friends, and yes, a few girlfriends. I just wanted something else with my life. The South was not for me."

"I get it, man. We all had our flying the coop times. Don't

sweat it. Besides, don't your bosses call you the deal slayer? You'll be out and back in a cool forty-eight."

"Yeah, it should be an easy deal," Dean admitted.

"See, it won't be so bad. Check out your alma matter, eat some fried seafood, get your signature and snag a flight home," Ray cheered.

Dean grinned, seeing a set roll in, "You're right. Tell you what, shortest ride in buys the drinks!"

Diving onto his board, Dean paddled into the power of the wave and pushed himself up. Hopping to his feet, he balanced his body and powered towards the shore.

Cleaned up from surfing, Dean and Ray both pulled their German convertibles up to the restaurant valet. Taking their slips, they headed into the building. Following a similarly attired crowd, they found the elevator.

In moments, the doors parting doors unveiled the evening sky and light lounge music streaming through the air. Greeted instantly by a hostess informing them that they were the fourth group in line for a table or, they could opt for standing spaces available on the patio.

Waving off the hostess, they made their way to a railing overlooking Hollywood and most of Los Angeles.

"So, the east coast...never been," Ray said.

"It's...it has its fine points. The water is warm. The seafood is great. The beaches are amazing," Dean said.

"And yet you couldn't wait to haul tail out of there," Ray said.

"*Anywhere*, at the time," Dean admitted.

Pausing their conversation, they gave their orders to a waitress who fluttered by their table.

"We all feel that way at some point. I peeled off for Baja right after I graduated. I landed in San Diego for a couple of years," Ray said.

"Not real far from home, you grew up in Irvine," Dean scoffed.

"Still, it's perspective," Ray shrugged.

The waitress stopped and handed the guys their martinis.

"Cheers," Dean lifted his glass.

"Cheers," Ray nodded, "To homecomings, whatever they may offer."

"Besides, LA has everything I need. Beaches, a great job, great people," Dean gave a nod to his friend.

"And the ladies," Ray grinned a childish grin.

For a moment, they took in the crowd. Ladies and gentlemen alike were in high polish - impeccable attire, well-coiffed, adorned with expensive jewelry and watches.

Noting the attractive crowd milling about the rooftop pool, Dean nodded. "Very true."

One of the ladies noticed that they had caught the eye of

the guys. Turning to face them, her pair of robust lips flashed a smile in their direction.

"And Botox," Dean said. "An awful lot of Botox."

"Augmented pretty is still pretty, right?" Ray asked, raising an eyebrow.

"I don't know," Dean sighed. "I'm not sure dating California style has worked out well for me."

"What about that girl Brianna? Whew, she was something," Ray suggested.

Dean shrugged, taking a sip of his martini, "She was okay. Felt like I constantly had to follow her around to her friends' parties and dinners. Never really connected just the two of us."

"How about Sophie? She was elegant."

"Sure, but if I had to hear about her last boyfriend's Ferrari or their trips to France one more time…."

"When you make partner, that could be you, buddy," Ray offered.

Dean shook his head, "I'm grateful that guy *wasn't* me. He was an expense account on two legs. No, thank you."

Ray swallowed a gulp of his martini. "The good news is, there is always a fresh stock of new potential future Mrs. Dean Taylors arriving daily. Maybe you just have to catch them before they turn."

Dean grinned, "Like Mary from Iowa?"

Ray winced, "Had to bring up Mary. She was so amazing

when we first dated. By our six-month anniversary, she was asking what *she* needed to be augmented."

He took a sip of his drink.

"I love the fact that she came to town in a half-broken down Chevrolet Malibu and complained about my three-year-old BMW," Ray said.

"In L.A. years that makes your car nearly a classic," Dean replied.

"Alright, alright. I grant you that in a city of over four million, finding 'the one' is a bit daunting. But you have got admit that the search is kind of fun," Ray grinned.

"I suppose," Dean's voice trailed off as his lips pressed into his martini glass.

Sorting his clothes for the trip and making neat piles on his bed, Dean laid out just enough for two days along with an outfit for traveling there. Nodding, he slid hangers into the garment bag for two suits and three shirts. Biting his lip, he decided to add a pair of shorts and a T-shirt, just in case.

He thought about adding a few more days' worth of clothes in the event his stay got extended, but decided he had to play to win with confidence. Besides, he reasoned, this way, he could carry everything on the plane and not have to check luggage. Dean preferred to travel light and agile.

Completing his packing, he grabbed his glass of sparkling

water and walked out to his patio. Leaning over his railing, he appreciated the Pacific breeze as he watched the Southern California life scroll past. There was never a shortage of people and activity. He laughed as he thought how funny it was that he was surrounded by so many people and yet, at times, felt strangely lonely.

Dean enjoyed his life in California. He advanced quickly in his career despite an endless supply of competition. Southern California was a place that embraced the entrepreneurial spirit and hard work, if, in exchange, it was a bit relentless.

Finishing his water, he headed in for the evening. Flights heading east meant an early wake-up call.

Chapter Three – Carolina Arrival

Flying directly into the Charlotte airport, despite being a four-hour drive from his ultimate destination, had a perk - an expanded selection of rental cars. Dean decided he was going to operate his trip in high style. Besides, the Charlotte airport had a lot more options for a quick departure when he had the deal wrapped up.

Navigating his way to the rental counter, he bypassed the line and headed to the VIP kiosk. "Mr. Taylor?" an attractive woman with mahogany skin asked as he approached.

Dean couldn't resist a smile, "I am."

"Your car is delivered to your left, and the air conditioner should be on and ready to for you, sir," the attendant said. "Would you like help with luggage, Mr. Taylor?"

Dean shook his head and thanked the attendant. Following her directions, he found a young man standing outside of a gleaming, champagne-colored Aston Martin convertible. The driver's door and trunk were open, and the young man silently took Dean's luggage and stowed it in the snug trunk. Lowering the lid, he found Dean already in the driver's seat.

Dean handed the young man a $fifty-dollar bill. "I believe the navigation is set for Wilmington already, sir."

"Thank you. I think I am ready to go."

"Very well. Enjoy your stay in North Carolina."

Like a child admiring his new toy at Christmas, Dean nodded, running his hand along the steering wheel. "This trip might not be so bad after all."

Putting the expensive luxury car into gear, the exhaust note let out a slight growl as Dean guided the vehicle toward the circular down ramp of the rental garage. Showing the guard his papers, he throttled the car as the gate swung up. Dean powered out of the airport and onto the expressway. He took advantage of the red light to lower the convertible roof and pulled his sunglasses out of his pocket.

Tapping the steering wheel, he let off the brake as the light changed guided the car onto Interstate 74 and began his drive east. Leaving Charlotte, Dean followed a steady stream of traffic through Monroe before the urban landscape gave way to the trees and hills of North Carolina's rural Piedmont.

Driving the powerful car with very little traffic through the rural highway was a treat for Dean, who was more used to the ever-constant traffic jams of Los Angeles. When saddled behind slower traffic, Dean took the opportunity to open the car up and sail quickly past. Despite driving past the Rockingham Speedway, he was surprised by the lack of urgency from drivers along the highway.

He glanced at the GPS on the dash. It showed he was somewhat ahead of schedule despite his encounter with the occasional slow vehicle. He settled in and elected to enjoy the late afternoon drive as he hurdled toward the coastal plains. He followed the stretch of road that mirrored the North and South Carolina border until he crossed over Interstate 95, where the state line dipped toward the south.

On this stretch of the trip, Dean could tell the difference in many of the cars. License plates noted travelers from a wide range of states, most cars packed with coolers, luggage, and the occasional surfboard as he closed in on the renowned beaches of the Carolinas.

The band of roads also triggered the deeper folds of Dean's mind to unpack flashes of memories. The ballfields of Whiteville and Lake Waccamaw. The turn-off where his family lived. Even the road with the pet cemetery where his childhood dog rested.

Passing the sign for Southport triggered images of the Fourth of July festival, walking along the waterfront where the Cape Fear River emptied into the Atlantic Ocean. The town was draped in patriotic bunting, each manicured home with gleaming white porches and pillars. The downtown area was closed to traffic so the Independence Day parade and visitors could wander unfettered. Dean could almost smell the blackpowder from the fireworks at night as the evening breeze drifted onshore. In flashes of blue and white and red, Dean could picture lying on a blanket with his girlfriend drinking in the night.

The pictures flew fast and furious, with a different face in the same scene. Chuckling smugly to himself, Dean admitted that he'd experienced that night year after year with a different girlfriend. Like sifting through snapshots, his mind rotated through the faces, pausing to let them find their place in his mental scrapbook. Most, especially the early ones, the innocent ones, conjured a smile. But as the images continued to come into focus, the final ones triggered a different response. Dean twisted in his seat, his nose wrinkled. Slices of pain pinged his chest. He winced as the dusty feeling of hurt and worse, guilt long forgotten were awakened, causing him to shake his head, trying to chase them away.

Stopping the cascade of memories, he shrugged them off as simple rites of passage, being young and impetuous in high school and then college. Closing in on Wilmington, Dean focused on the GPS and the route to his rental house. Passing the USS North Carolina Battleship memorialized across the Cape Fear River from downtown Wilmington, Dean followed the instructions from the route guidance voice over the car stereo, wrapping around the town and toward the beaches.

Skirting downtown, his path led him from the Market Street exit and then onto College Drive, taking him past the main entrance for the University of North Carolina at Wilmington. Despite how glad he was to graduate and leave the campus for the last time, he couldn't resist a smile as his convertible sped past.

Pulling up to a red light just beyond the school, he guided the Aston Martin to stop. A raised, Bondo-speckled pick-up truck blaring country music revved its engine, a stream of black smoke billowing from its massive exhaust. The growl of the Aston competed well against the burl of the raised pickup at the stoplight.

The driver grinned at Dean as he spat out of his window. Dean pressed a button on his steering wheel, nudging the volume on his music, shaking his head. When the light turned green, he let the big truck roar maddeningly off the line before letting off his brakes and slamming his foot on the accelerator. The truck was no match for the powerful luxury car. The convertible shot forward allowing Dean to quickly merge in front of the pick-up as he swung toward the Wrightsville Beach exit. Passing a police officer as he made the merge, Dean let off the gas and offered an apologetic wave as he pursed his lips.

Dean studied his rearview mirror for a moment, before guiding the convertible towards the Atlantic Ocean. The gentle rise of the bridge that crossed the Intracoastal Waterway cresting in the mimosa-colored night sky soared over boats that left soft white streaks in their wake. The backdrop of the Atlantic eclipsed the fantastic view with its narrow strip of land and sandy beaches. Dean couldn't stifle a feeling of adoration. This was a part of North Carolina he had and would always appreciate.

Pulling onto the oceanfront drive of Wrightsville Beach, Dean headed for the beach house his company rented for his stay. Passing the surf shops, beach stores, and the restaurants offered the excitement that beach towns provide.

Passing rows of tall beachfront houses clad in soft coastal colors, he found the number on his GPS. Pulling the Aston Martin under the house built high on stilts, he raised the convertible top and grabbed his scant luggage.

Walking up the steps of the house led his gaze towards the shoreline and over the dunes, providing a commanding view of the beach and ocean before he ever stepped foot in the immaculate beachfront home.

Opening the door, Dean tossed his luggage down. Crossing through the living area to the massive set of French doors, he flung them open, letting the ocean air and crashing waves permeate the house. Despite himself, a moment of adoration and deep satiation overwhelmed him. Taking a moment to drink in the view, the feel of the breeze against his face, and the smells of the ocean, Dean froze in front of the open doors.

After several long moments, he snapped out of his glorious

daze and took in the rest of the house. Carrying his luggage into the master suite, he deposited it on a bench and retreated to the main room.

Eyeing a welcome basket set by the management company, he pilfered it for snacks and a bottle of wine. Wasting no time, he opened the wine and filled a glass. Grabbing his laptop, he settled into an Adirondack chair on the patio overlooking the beach as he looked over his notes for his meeting the next day.

Putting the wineglass to his lips and looking over the top of his laptop notes, the Atlantic and the colors of that evening sky played off the incoming surf entranced Dean. The melody of the waves crashing against the sand was sweet music as he reveled in the scene.

Dean woke the next morning with a slight start. Glancing at the clock, he found the he had beat his alarm by several minutes. The morning sun had slowly risen above the horizon, the light nudging Dean awake. Laying back, he listened to the morning surf roll in against the sand. Propping his head up, he studied the vast array of blues outside of the open master suite double French doors.

As his alarm went off, he hit the cancel button and rolled out of bed. Shuffling toward the bedroom patio, he plopped down in one of the padded chairs that faced the ocean. Stretching his legs, he leaned back and allowed himself to slowly wake up to the symphony and visual display of the Carolina coast.

The ocean breeze was refreshing, and despite the three-hour difference, he felt fantastic. Still, he decided to hunt down an espresso. Ready to tackle the day, Dean wanted to get the meeting underway and wrapped up so he could close the deal and return to his own life in California.

Firing up the Aston Martin, he lowered the top and backed out of the driveway. Cruising along the oceanfront boulevard, in the morning, with the sun barely crested and the Atlantic breeze streaming by, Dean was nearly in bliss. Despite all of his blustering, he couldn't help but to be completely enamored with his current state at that exact place and time.

Following his GPS' instructions over the car's speakers, he found a little coffee shop not far from his rental. Across from a breakfast restaurant, he watched families head in, ready to get an early start on their beach adventures. Walking into the little coffee shop, the scent of freshly roasted and ground coffee met him as he opened the screen door.

"Hey," a vibrant voice drawled from behind the counter.

Dean smiled at the young barista. "Good morning."

"What can I get you?"

Dean wrinkled his nose slightly, "You have almond milk?"

"Uh, no," the barista frowned.

"That's okay. How about a cappuccino?"

"Cinnamon?"

"Yes, please," Dean nodded.

As the barista began working on his beverage, she asked above the whir of the machinery, "You here with your family?"

Dean shook his head, "Nope, here on business."

"Oh," the barista frowned again. "That's too bad."

"It's alright. I like my job."

"Oh, I didn't mean it exactly like that. Just a shame to waste a perfectly good day at the beach working the whole time."

Dean grinned, "Yeah, I guess you're right."

"You been here before?"

"Yeah. I grew up not far from here. I went to college in Wilmington," Dean admitted.

The barista stopped what she was doing and studied Dean for a solid moment. "No way."

"Way," Dean chuckled.

"Where do you live now?" the barista asked and then backtracked, "I mean, if you want to share, don't mean to be nosy."

"That's alright. I live in Southern California now. Haven't been back in…about ten years, until now."

"Wow. Things changed a bunch?"

Dean laughed, "A bit."

"You miss it? North Carolina, I mean. It's kind of home, right?"

Dean bit his lip, evaluating his answer. "I miss the beach, but really, I was ready for something new. I left three days after I graduated and never looked back."

"Until now."

"Until now."

"Wow. That's crazy," the barista pressed as she worked on Dean's coffee. "You must have family and friends here?"

"Not really. I mean, I am sure some friends from high school and college might still be around, but most of my family moved away for one reason or another."

"Oh," the barista nodded handing Dean his cappuccino. "I hope you find some time to enjoy the beach while you're here. It's what you missed, after all. I get that. I *looove* the beach."

Dean stuffed a wad of bills in the tip jar on the counter, "Thank you."

"Bye, maybe we'll see you again," the barista said.

Dean backed out of the coffee shop, sliding through the screen door, holding it open for a couple who were heading in. Taking a sip of his coffee, he opened the driver's door of his rental car and slid into the driver's seat. Bringing the car to life, he headed back to the beach house.

Dean rooted through the welcome basket in the kitchen of the rental, pulling out some blueberries and a granola bar. Carrying his coffee and his foraged breakfast, he settled back in one of the patio chairs on the massive back porch overlooking the beach.

An occasional beachcomber hunting for shells or early

morning joggers would pass by. Finishing his breakfast, he glanced at his phone. Noting the time, he realized he had room for a morning run. Eschewing his running shoes, Dean donned the one pair of shorts he packed and skipped down the steps in his bare feet.

Walking down the long, private wooden walkway that traversed the dunes, he marched to the beach. Jogging through the warming, soft and dry sand, he headed for the semi-firm sand that the tide had recently worked smooth. Each footfall left an impression as he glided by.

Working his way down the beach, he would occasionally veer away from the surf as the rogue stray wave crept further ashore.

In the distance, he spied Crystal Pier as a goal for him to reach passing shells and full sand dollars. He grinned as he pressed a solid pace in the fresh morning air. Seagulls and sandpipers played along the shore in front of him, scampering a swath around him as he ran by.

Occasionally, he would run onto the softer sand higher up the beach to circumnavigate a fisherman casting a line out into the surf. Along one stretch, half a dozen surfers made their way into the morning breakers.

When he made it to Crystal Pier, he slowed and turned to head back. The morning sun met with humidity and accelerated the day's heat in a way he was not used to living in California.

Slowing to a brief stop, he kicked at the frothy breakwater. Spinning about-face, he began a jog back over his track in the sand. The beach was slowly coming to life as families started to walk out from their beach houses or the access areas.

Making it back to his walkway, he couldn't resist veering towards the waves. He leaped over the breakers, gliding into the surf. Swimming out past the break, he floated in the swells. Kicking his feet gently to stay atop of the water.

After bobbing through several sets of waves, he chose one to swim along with, allowing it to carry him ashore. Grinning, he pushed back to the walkway. He couldn't resist at least jumping into the Atlantic while he was so close. He had to admit that the water felt fantastic- instantly tolerable versus the chilly Pacific. Besides, who knew when, if ever, he would swim at the Carolina coast ever again. Jogging up his walkway, he headed in for a shower.

Chapter Four - Cape Fear

Wheeling the Aston down Oleander Drive and heading downtown, Dean made his way to his meeting. As he drove through town, he was impressed with the city's growth since he left. There were some modern touches, but Wilmington had not relinquished any of its classic feel or southern charm.

Dean found his prospective client in a remodeled building perched a few blocks uphill from the Cape Fear River, a converted home with a massive, two-story wrap around porch. The upper floors were peeking over magnolia trees that afforded a view of the river. As he strode up the porch steps, each footfall sang his presence with the creaky wood. He tried the handle and found it locked.

Glancing at his watch, Dean admitted he was ten minutes early, but still, he expected someone to be there. Resigning himself to the circumstance, he walked to the porch and perched with one leg hoisted on the porch rail, the other firmly planted on the decking.

Pulling out his phone, he called the office number; it rang through to the recorded answering system. Cycling through the emails on his cellphone, he found the contact information for the CEO. Clicking the phone number in the email signature, he waited.

"Good morning, this is Bart Stevens."

"Mr. Stevens, this is Dean Taylor. I am at your office. I just wanted to ensure that we were still on for our meeting this morning."

"Well, sure we are, but it ain't that time yet. I'll be there in a bit, and Charlotte should be there momentarily to let you in and make sure you are comfortable."

"Thank you, Mr. Stevens, I will see you shortly." Dean closed out of his phone and stared at it for a moment. Most of his deals met with a sense of urgency. Mr. Stevens did not appear to be in any such rush.

Resigned to waiting, Dean thumbed through the messages on his phone. Since he was three hours ahead, no one was in the office. The Cape Fear account was his only current East Coast deal with Dana Holdings. He sighed, unable to make positive use of his time. He forced himself to relax and watch the town of Wilmington bloom to life for the day.

The morning sun mixed with the coastal Carolina humidity elicited beads of sweat forming on Dean's forehead as he waited on the porch. He was glad that he had foregone the tie, but the suit was becoming oppressive. Just as he feared losing the crispness he levied for the presentation, a pleasant woman with a slight bouffant hairstyle approached the steps, keys jingling in her hand.

"Well, you must be Mr. Taylor. Prompt, I see. Well, come on, let's get you inside."

Dean followed the woman into the building. "Thank you, Ms...?"

The woman giggled, "Just Charlotte will do fine. May I get you some iced tea or a Pepsi?"

"Water would be great."

"Very well. You'll be meeting in the Masonboro Room behind those double doors. Make yourself at home."

Dean opened the doors and selected a seat with his back to the wall so that he could observe those coming down the hall. Keeping his presentation simple, he slid a single folder out of his bag and placed it in front of him. As Charlotte delivered his water, she smiled and left him so that she could handle the phones while busily watering the flowers around the office.

Knowing the contents of the folder by heart, he mindlessly thumbed through the documents as he waited. Glancing at his watch, he determined he could wrap things up and be on the 3 p.m. flight and return home with a signature intact.

Around the meeting room were classic pictures of Wilmington. Black and white images of the city and its industry along the Cape Fear River, long before every household owned a car and interstates connected towns.

The pictures of downtown seemed simple and quaint.

The river scenes with dockworkers unloading boats laden depicted how much the river influenced the city.

Pictures of the beaches were even starker with a vibrant and festive boardwalk giving way to miles of undeveloped beachfront.

Dean's spell of nostalgia shattered with the creaking front door and booming, jolly voice.

As Bart Stevens burst into the office, Dean could hear him boisterously greet Charlotte and comment on the Azaleas she added to the office lobby.

"Mr. Taylor is waiting for you in the Masonboro Room."

"Great, I will be right in after I drop my things off in my office. Will you send Jacob and Chester in there as well?"

"Of course," Charlotte sang.

Dean straightened his packet as he sat up tall in his seat. Hands folded on the folders in front of him, he waited for Mr. Stevens and his associates to join him. Tapping at the table, Dean took a sip of his water. Waiting further, he pushed back from the table and laid a leg over his knee, and his folded hands migrated to his lap. Waiting.

Moments after squirming into his new position, two young

men entered the conference room, each dressed business casual though clad with expensive brands. Introducing themselves, they each took a seat leaving an empty chair between them.

Shortly after, Bart Stevens entered and took the seat that was saved for him. With a beaming smile and an outstretched hand, he greeted Dean. "So, I understand you were a Seahawk."

"Yessir, I was. Business degree at UNCW and then MBA and JD in California."

"Excellent, my boy went to Duke, but to tell you that truth, always been a Tarheel at heart myself."

Chester Stevens shot a look, "Really, Dad?"

"That's why I hired Jacob to work with you. He even has what I believe is a Carolina blue shirt. I like it," Stevens grinned in approval.

"Well, Mr. Stevens, I appreciate you taking the meeting. It sounds like, according to our phone conversations and review of the documents, we should be in excellent shape. Dana Holdings would love to welcome Cape Fear Commercial into our family. I think you will see from our projections that with the inclusion of Cape Fear's clients and resources, we have adjusted the PE ratio in your favor." Whipping out a thick stack of contract papers, Dean spun them around to face Stevens. "A few signatures and initials, that yacht you mentioned as a retirement gift and, as we discussed, Chester's appointment as VP of the Cape Fear Division of Dana Holdings is all set."

Stevens studied the documents Dean laid out before him. "This...all looks great. I appreciate the increased P/E ratio, and the graphs look fantastic." Sighing, Stevens crossed his fingers with his hands resting on top of the documents and looked intently across the table at Dean. "Cape Fear Commercial is more than growth numbers and charts and real estate. It is people, a legacy. If you are going to take over Cape Fear, I need you to see it in action. Get to know the people. I am satisfied with our arrangement for my gain, even for Chester's future. But I need you to interact with Jacob and Charlotte and the people at the Hanover facility and in Holly Vale and North Side…"

Dean looked a mix of puzzled and perturbed. "Sir, our intentions have been clear. Outside of a few redundant C-suite and administrative personnel, we are leaving the workers and management intact. I am sure we can make arrangements to ensure that Jacob is part of the executive organization as well."

"Son, I know you say that now, and I believe your intentions. I do. But I also know the first quarter that actuals fall short of projections, numbers will be adjusted, and the easiest way to adjust those numbers is through headcount and locations. If you want this deal, I need you to spend some time here, look at each facility with your own eyes, and understand its impact on the community. I need you to look into the faces of the employees and understand that their families rely on them. Now, I know you are not the final decision maker, but I need someone at Dana

Holdings headquarters some 3,000 miles away to carry the voice of the people at Cape Fear Commercial here in North Carolina." Scooting his chair back from the table, he looked calm and pleasant and silent at Dean awaiting his response.

Holding in a sigh, noting that his 3 pm flight idea had just been pronounced dead, Dean forced a smile. "It would be my pleasure, and in truth, I would not have it any other way."

"Great!" Stevens beamed. "Let's get you started tomorrow. The guys, Charlotte and I have some plans to put together. Chester will send you an itinerary by the end of the day. Enjoy your day in North Carolina, Mr. Taylor."

Dean's calm façade was feigned as the next steps of the process wouldn't even begin until the next day. "I look forward to Chester's communication and visiting the fine people at your plants, Mr. Stevens."

Pushing his chair away from the table, Dean shook each man's hands and gathered up his papers. Trying to hide his dejection and frustration, he forced a smile and walked out of the meeting room and into the lobby. With a nod of his head, he said, "Thank you, Ms. Charlotte."

"My pleasure, Mr. Taylor. Enjoy your day in North Carolina. Let me know if there is anything I can do for you during your stay. As you know, North Carolina is fantastic this time of year," the receptionist beamed.

"Indeed, it is," Dean mumbled half-heartedly.

Walking around the sidewalk and to the driver's side door of his car, he let out a deep breath, his mind reeling, fighting for how the process of this deal was supposed to take place. In most meetings, he held the upper hand. Mr. Stevens seemed to have his course of action set and was not hearing any other plausible path.

"Kudos to him," Dean chuckled to himself. Suddenly, he realized the affable entrepreneur might just be shrewder than he had been given credit for being.

Dean fired up the Aston Martin. Tossing his jacket in the back seat and rolling up his shirt sleeves, he lowered the roof and slipped on his sunglasses. The engine came to life, and Dean pushed hard on the gas pedal, encouraging the V12 engine to roar, propelling the luxury car onto the road.

Dejected and steaming, he throttled hard, struggling to keep within ten miles an hour of the speed limit. As he left Wilmington towards the beach, Dean figured at least he had the afternoon to catch up on calls and emails for other proposals he had been working negotiating.

His music was interrupted by his cell phone that synched through the car stereo. Dean's boss' voice called out over the speakers. "Well, do you have signatures in hand?"

Dean winced as he throttled down so that he could hear better, "Not quite, essentially a done deal, but…" He went on to fill in his boss on Steven's demands.

"Sounds reasonable. A few hoops to jump through, but

you've got this. Just reassure Stevens that the people will be protected, at least until the ink dries..." Marshall Givings chided. "Look, you might as well catch up with friends while you are there. Relax today, close it out tomorrow. You'll be on a flight with signature in hand tomorrow night."

"Yessir," Dean acknowledged and thumbed the switch to end the call.

Dean's conversation with Marshall did little to improve his spirit. He was more focused than ever to push through the day with catch-up work at the rental beach house.

Chapter Five –

The Brighter, Sandier Side of Delays

Holing up in the beach house, Dean had his laptop worked to a frenzy. He was managing his California based team from afar, finessing his outstanding deals, and reaching out to leads that had compiled that he had not had time to work while closing the last contract. Hours had passed as he tried to while away the day.

Out of the window of his makeshift office, he watched the afternoon swells turn into overhead break. His mind flashed to the surfboards he had seen displayed in the mudroom off the entry. Seeing a handful of surfers dot the calm past the breakers, he rubbed his face, feeling he was up against a wall for progress on his work.

Dean reasoned that he could stand to get some air and refresh himself to continue the work onslaught. Perhaps some saltwater and exercise would serve to clear his head. Pushing away from the desk, he dug into his luggage and found the swim trunks he packed in case he found a pool for laps and threw them on. Snatching a board from its perch, he headed down the private boardwalk past the dunes and onto the beach.

In an almost childlike uninhibited exuberance, Dean's pace increased to a near sprint as he launched himself into the surf and over the first breaker. Launching his belly onto the board, he glided on top of the water. Leaning on the front of the board and diving under the next set of waves, popping up, he swam his arms on either side of the board, propelling himself past the waves until he reached the calmer water of the undulating swells.

Sitting atop his board, he watched the surfers a few hundred yards down the beach and studied the rides they were taking to judge the sets. Looking out toward the horizon, he patiently observed the oncoming waves. Seeing the first wave pop and then the second, he eyed the third, spaced far enough from the first two not to be lost in their wash, yet close enough to benefit from their rise. He selected it.

Facing the beach, he let the first wave roll by and then the second. He had a moment of doubt as that wave felt good, and then he focused on preparing for the third. As the swell began to trough, Dean paddled hard as the third wave roared under him. Urging the board to race to the tip of the curl as it crested, Dean launched himself upwards, landing his feet on the surface of the board, bending at the knees to achieve maximum balance. He shifted his weight slightly to his back foot, allowing the nose of the board to rise. He used his planted foot to pivot the board in a position to maximize the power of the wave as it carried Dean toward the shore.

Sliding left and right, Dean extended his ride as far as he felt the wave's momentum would carry him. Feeling the breeze against his face, the unreal feeling of the power of the ocean below as it brought him forward while exhilarating was strangely peaceful at the same time, as long as the ride lasted.

Baling to the side when he felt the power wane, stranded the board in the wash of the immense break. Dean shot out of the water and smoothed his hair back, swiping the saltwater from his face. He grinned triumphantly. As desperate as he was to move away from North Carolina, the beach had seared its power, beauty and grace into Dean's heart. The surf awakened a feeling, a youthfulness he had not recalled in quote some time.

After several rides, Dean walked ashore with a bounce in his step. As much as he struggled to fit in North Carolina, the Atlantic was his playground and a permanent feeling of home to him. Walking back to the rental house, Dean had a fresh perspective on the day.

Showering off the sand and salt, he couldn't think of anything better than dropping the top on the Aston and hunting down a storied plate of East Coast seafood for dinner.

The Crystal Pier was not far from Dean's beach house, but he had a recollection of it as a great place to eat with endless ocean views. Pulling the Aston Martin into the parking lot, Dean searched for the valet. Confounded when he didn't find one, he circled the parking lot. Each spot was full during the busy dinner hour of the summer tourist season. Circling the lot not once, or twice, but three times, he relented to finding street parking a few blocks away. Nervously pulling the $200,000 vehicle alongside the road against the curb of the sidewalk, he shut off the engine. Dean looked back multiple times to assess the safety of the rental car, ultimately relenting to leave the vehicle to fate, he reluctantly headed for the restaurant.

As he marched up the steps, two heavy doors were heaved open with two young, smiling blondes welcoming him with sharp southern accents. Dean pulled off his sunglasses as he nodded his appreciation and entered the restaurant. Finding the hostess, he elected to be seated on the pier extending over the waves. A calypso band played softly at the end of the restaurant's portion of the dock as families hauled fishing poles and buckets to the very end.

The hostess presented Dean with a seat overlooking the water. Sitting back, he soaked in the view. His table straddled the section of the beach where the waves met the sand. It was a perfect spot on a near-perfect evening. It was still warm out, but the evening onshore breeze had begun to whisper.

Dean barely noticed when a water glass set before him. Taken by the early evening beach scene, the changes of colors in the sky, and the waves as the sun yielded its presence on the day, Dean was broken out of his trance by a soft southern voice.

"Good evening, sir. May I get you some tea or a glass of wine?" Dean looked up at the owner of the voice. A woman roughly his age stood in front of him, a server's tray perched against her hip.

Her skin was delicately sun-kissed, freckles playfully accenting her cheeks. Her sun and saltwater influenced blonde hair was chopped to her shoulders, framing her face. Dean studied her deep blue eyes, which were distant and veiled. They reminded him of how he assumed when he looked off during his boardroom negotiations.

Dean noticed she didn't look directly at him when she spoke, but instead in the vicinity of him. She pursed her lips a bit impatiently. Catching herself, she relaxed them into a feigned smile.

Shaking himself, Dean asked for a glass of pinot gris. In an instant, she whisked herself away and onto her next table before skittering off toward the kitchen.

His focus settling back on the beach and evening surf, he absently reached for the glass of wine that set down quickly as the waitress rushed off to attend another table. The crisp wine was a perfect complement to the atmosphere and evening.

The waitress again summoned Dean's attention. "Are you ready to order?" her eyes barely met his before darting off towards the beach in a distant gaze.

"What do you recommend?"

The waitress' pleasant visage failed to hide her distance, if not annoyance. "The clams royale is a customer favorite. The mahi mahi is great. Really, everything is good. I wouldn't go with the chicken. You could get that almost anywhere." Despite herself, she managed a half-smile with her remark.

Dean's return smile broadened her's if only for a moment.

Ordering the mahi mahi, he handed over his menu. He remembered eating Mahi all the time when he lived in North Carolina. His best friend's dad would often take boat trips between Wrightsville Beach and Cape Hatteras and come back with spectacular fish, inviting their families together for a barbecue.

When his dish arrived, Dean straightened up, thanked the waitress, and bowed his head for a moment before diving into his food. The waitress cocked her head slightly as she observed the restaurant's guest.

Dean dug into his plate of expertly cooked fish with vigor. There was a subtle difference in how the east and west coasts prepared seafood; he appreciated both. Pacific seafood was simple, clean, and light. Atlantic seafood had a deeper, richer flavor and presentation. With this sample in front of him, he had to give the nod to the Atlantic preparation.

The waitress stopped by to check on his food, ready to whisk away before there was an opportunity for a genuine answer.

"It's great, thank you. I can see why you recommended it," Dean replied.

"It's one of the favorites…" she shrugged.

"I'm sorry I didn't catch your name."

A deeply guarded look crossed her face, she hesitated before she replied softly, "Shelby. My name is Shelby."

"Well, thank you, Shelby. Dinner was great, as was the service," Dean said.

Nodding, Shelby bolted away. After a few steps, she spun and came back. "Why was the service so great?" she questioned, her hands dropping to her hips as if she was expecting some forward response.

"I like the fact that you were just attentive enough, yet left me to my thoughts and the opportunity to enjoy my meal with the amazing backdrop afforded by being here on the pier," Dean replied calmly.

"Oh. I see. Well, thank you," the waitress said curtly and then abruptly turned and went on with her duties.

Dean watched her with a raised eyebrow. Shrugging, he took a sip of wine and returned to enjoy the rest of his meal.

As Dean left the restaurant, he enjoyed the cooler night air as he returned to his rented convertible, his belly adequately satiated. After a brief inspection, he was satisfied the valet-less luxury car was as he left it. Dropping the top, he fired up the engine and pulled away from the curb.

Driving along the coastal road, snaking between rows of hoses and the occasional hotel, Dean arrived back at the beach house. Walking up the steps and hearing the waves crash in the night less than a hundred yards away was a welcome greeting.

As he entered the house, he opened the sets of French doors as he had the evening before letting the night breeze and ocean symphony serenade him to sleep.

Chapter Six –
"Hello, I'm Your Past. I'll be your Guide Today."

D ean woke up hopeful that the day's activities would finally close the deal, and he could get back to California and his life. Putting on his suit, he grabbed a leather notebook, stuffed the contract in it, and headed out of the door.

He begrudgingly elected to keep the convertible top in place. Pulling out of the parking space under the stilts of the beach house he accelerated on to the road toward Wilmington. Stopping at the same coffee shop as day before, he exchanged brief pleasantries with the barista, again, and ended up holding the door open for the same couple.

Feeling good about the day, Dean had a bounce in his step. He was glad to be back in work mode, ready to take action. That was when he felt most confident, most in control.

Navigating the drive from Wrightsville Beach again to the

big white house that Cape Fear Commercial used as its administrative building, Dean parked purposely out front so that the employees would see the Aston Martin on their way to work. Proceeding up the steps, he again perched on the porch railing, waiting for Charlotte and Mr. Stevens to arrive.

As Dean waited, he wondered if he would be traveling the sites with Chester or Jacob. Scrolling through his emails, he sipped his cappuccino.

A voice, vaguely familiar, broke his concentration. "Dean? Dean Taylor? Oh, my, when Mr. Stevens said I was going to escort Mr. Taylor to our facilities, I never imagined it would be you."

Dean's head flashed with images from his past. In seconds, first dates, first kisses, walks on the beach, a break-up, and a woman in tears filled his mind. "Cassie Sutton," Dean acknowledged through bewildered eyes and reddened cheeks.

Cassie smiled, giving Dean a once-over, "It looks like we'll be spending the day together."

"Wow, I mean, it's been a long time," Dean stuttered.

"Yes, it has. I don't think anyone around here has seen or heard from you since graduation."

Before Dean could respond, a voice beamed coming up from the sidewalk, "You two have met. Fantastic."

"Mr. Stevens," Dean said, willing his cheeks to return to the proper temperature. "I am looking forward to meeting the folks at your facilities. Will we be reconvening later this afternoon?"

"Perhaps. We'll see how your day goes with Ms. Sutton. I find her perspective quite valuable," Mr. Stevens smiled.

"Excellent," Dean sighed.

Turning to Cassie, Dean asked, "Well, shall we?"

"I'm ready," Cassie nodded. Glancing at the curb, she added, "You might want to park your convertible outback. It is a little flashy for visiting the hardworking people at the manufacturing and warehouse sites. We can take my SUV. It will fit in a little better."

Stymied, Dean complied and found the little parking area for the office around the block. Cassie pulled alongside in her SUV and rolled down the passenger window. "Hop in," she grinned.

Dean couldn't be sure, but Cassie seemed to be relishing being in control of the experience and having an influence over whether Dean got his deal inked or not.

Reluctantly, he climbed into her passenger seat, hands clasped on top of the leather portfolio he placed on his lap. "Well… this will be fun."

Cassie laughed, "Certainly will be an *interesting* day. Buckle up."

Pulling out of the driveway and onto the road, she began their drive to the first facility.

"So, you are the…," Dean started.

"Public Relations Director," Cassie stated, "And key

evaluator of outsiders."

"Right. I'm an outsider, now."

"Oh, you are most *certainly* an outsider," Cassie laughed, wheeling the SUV down the road.

Dean sat silently, stewing in his predicament. A rare situation he did not know how to manage.

"Where have you been all of these years? You've done okay for yourself."

"I moved to California, got my post-graduate work in and have been working in asset evaluation, negotiation and purchasing for one of the biggest acquisition companies in the country," Dean replied.

"So, this company you work for…they don't actually make anything, design, manufacture…,"

Dean shook his head, "No, not really. They consult, influence all of those activities as well as in all aspects of running a company– management, employee strategies and benefits, marketing and distribution, at times… liquidation."

"I see," Cassie replied thoughtfully. "Mr. Stevens was concerned you were a love 'em and leave 'em kind of company."

Dean's cheeks returned to white-hot and bright red. "About…"

Before he could get a word out, they wheeled into the parking lot of the first facility in New Hanover County.

"We're here," Cassie sang cheerfully.

Dean was more sure than ever that Cassie was enjoying every moment of the day's events with the power she wielded as to its conclusion.

"So, what's the plan?" Dean asked, getting out of the SUV.

"We mingle."

Dean nodded slowly and muttered, "Right. Mingle."

"Aw, c'mon, it will be fun!"

Having arrived along with most of the morning shift workers, Dean and Cassie merged with the flow. Dean quietly observed as they walked. He watched a wide variety of people make their way to work. Some were dropped off by spouses with kisses goodbye and toddlers waving from rear windows. Others arrived in a whole manner of vehicles. Raised four-wheel-drive trucks, minivans, and family sedans found their way into the parking lot.

Mixing in with the crowd, most workers met up with a colleague while they walked into the plant together. The conversations centered around their families– planned vacations, teenagers, and in-laws.

Ahead of them, a small group walked in a close huddle. "Did you hear that they are finally looking at selling?"

"What? I've already started my retirement countdown. What happens now?"

One of his colleagues gave him a light shove, "You have like twelve years left."

"Eleven. Still, the clock starts all over when they shut this place down."

"Who says they are going to shut anything down?"

"That's what they do. Call it "downsizing" or some other fancy term. All it means to the worker like us is a loss of a paycheck and everything we've worked for."

"Stevens wouldn't allow that…would he?"

"Would you sell your house?"

"What do you mean?"

"If someone knocked on your door and said they wanted to buy it today, would you sell it?"

"No. My wife would kill me."

"What if they offered a million dollars?"

"Then I'd take it. Because for that, my wife would kill me if I *didn't* take it."

"Right. That's what will happen with Stevens. They'll offer a dollar that even he couldn't refuse."

"I guess. It just doesn't seem like the boss."

"Just isn't right."

"Face it, boys. We are all just cogs in the machine."

Raising a thermos in a toast, another said, "Well, here's to cogs!"

Cassie shot Dean a look over the exchange. Dean answered back with a shrug as if to say it wasn't his call.

Throughout the morning, Dean met with plant managers

and key staff. Occasionally, Cassie would bring Dean to a floor worker running a machine, stacking heavy boxes, or carefully inspecting a part or finished product.

When they had covered most of the facility, Cassie led him out of the plant and to the parking lot.

"So, what do you think?"

"Well, given the age of the facility, it is great shape. Most of the key equipment looks new and updated," Dean noted.

"I meant about the *people*," Cassie replied sternly.

"Well, yeah. I was getting there. The employees are hardworking, knowledgeable, care about each other…."

"They do care about each other, and we care about them. That is *why* Cape Fear employees work so hard," Cassie said.

"Yeah, that and a paycheck," Dean scoffed.

"That's just it. Our employees have signed up for more than a paycheck…," Cassie argued. "This mission that Mr. Stevens has you on is to help you understand just that."

"I know that. I am just saying it is a factor. When taking over a company, there are three ways to manage personnel. You can reduce the higher salaried employees for more, lower waged employees. You can slim down the number of employees but pay those you keep more. The least preferred is to automate or outsource some of those roles. Limit cost and overhead as much as possible," Dean shared.

"And what is your plan here?" Cassie demanded.

"Well, I wouldn't worry too much about automation or outsourcing. The reason why Dana Holdings is interested is there are not a lot of companies out there that do exactly what you do. That is strongly in favor of keeping the vast majority of Cape Fear Commercial intact."

"Well, that's good to hear." Glancing at her watch, she said, "We have a lot of ground to cover today, but what do you say we go to lunch in between here and our next stop?"

"I could eat," Dean smiled.

Cassie swung her SUV into a gravel parking lot for a café that sat along the Cape Fear River. "How long has it been since you had good Carolina barbecue and hush puppies?"

"It's been a while," Dean admitted.

Walking across the porch and into the café, Cassie led him to a table on the back deck hanging just over the river's edge. A "Don't Feed the Alligators" sign was pinned securely to the deck rail.

Sitting on either side of the red gingham clad tabletop, they waited for a waitress to bring them some tea and take their orders.

"So," Dean started and shifted in his seat. "About how we...I left things. I probably could have done that better."

Cassie let out a howl of laughter. "You think? We were supposed to go to my parents that weekend for my sister's engagement announcement dinner. Instead, I had you standing outside of my dorm door clearly not packed for a trip. Instead, you casually explained that you weren't going, and you were breaking up with me."

"Yeah," Dean looked at the table cloth, sheepishly, "That probably wasn't right."

"Oh, on top of that, I come back to school Sunday night to learn that you hooked up Shari what's-her-face."

Dean bobbed his head, "Well, hooked up is a bit strong…"

"Hooked up, dated, whatever. And how about Shari? She didn't last long. The weekend after that it was Susie Baxter. At least she lasted a little while. Until Betsy Lee came along," Cassie laughed. With a mischievous grin, she teases, "At least, *she* threw you for one, huh?"

Dean looked down, "Yeah. Betsy Lee…she, uh, that one hurt a bit."

"You would have thought that experience would have slowed you down. Not long after Betsy Lee was Christine Longmire. Cute girl, Christine," Cassie reflected.

"Wow, you really paid attention…and counted," Dean said softly, rubbing his neck nervously.

"Truth is Dean; you were likable. You weren't *not* a gentleman. I don't mean that in any way. But when you were ready to move on, ouch, you ripped that band-aid off and were gone."

"I'm sorry. I didn't mean to hurt you," Dean admitted solemnly.

"I know that. You *did* hurt me, though. I get that relationships end. But have some nuance to it, you know? Wait a bit before you twist the knife to see you walking another girl to class three days later."

"Yeah," Dean bobbed his head.

"So, back at you. Is that how you are going to play this purchase? Be charming. Have a few good times and show up at the door letting the workers know their jobs are gone?" Cassie demanded.

"No."

"Better not," Cassie said, sitting back as the waitress laid down two barbecue plates and basket of hush puppies. "Alright, let's eat!"

She switched gears from serious interrogation to gleefully working into her food so abruptly, that it caused Dean to pause for a moment before shrugging and diving into his plate.

"You know, this stuff is pretty good," Dean admitted taking a forkful of barbecue pork from the discarded buns of his sandwich.

Cassie eyed him with an air of suspicion as she held her now sandwich in her hand. "That how they eat sandwiches in California?"

"Oh, I don't eat carbs much," Dean explained.

"Hmm," Cassie offered as she took another bite of her sandwich. "You sure don't make a very good southern boy."

Dean creased his brows, "That's why I left."

"So, what's it like out there, anyways, California?"

"It's nice. Busy. Lots of people *everywhere*. But it's a good lifestyle. The sun always shines. Business gets done. I like it," Dean replied.

"Well, I'm glad you're happy."

"Thank you," Dean raised his iced tea to cheers Cassie.

As he sipped, he scrunched his face. "Ugh, I wonder if they have unsweetened..."

Finished with lunch, Cassie and Dean headed further out of town. They left the road mirroring the Cape Fear River and followed I-40, where the cities grew smaller and further apart. Ultimately, Cassie turned off an exit ramp and meandered down a rural highway until it ran through a quiet little town. White fences surrounded squares of lawns. Little more than a church, a gas station, school, and a single store graced the main avenue.

Pushing beyond the outskirts of the town, they reached the drive for the second facility. As Cassie pulled into a parking space, Dean observed the grounds. The landscape was impressively well kept with bushes cut into tidy rows. The building itself showed its age, but was otherwise in presentable shape.

As they walked into the plant, the plant manager immediately greeted Cassie and Dean. "Welcome to the Holly Vale plant. Let's...let's show you around."

"Dean, this is Marty Davis. He has been the plant manager for eleven years," Cassie introduced the nervous man.

"I've been a Cape Fear Commercial employee for thirty-three years. Ccan you believe it?" Marty shared.

"Wow, that's very impressive. The whole time at this site?"

"Yes, started right of high school. Mr. Stevens paid for me to attend community college, and I moved my way up," Marty said.

"That is excellent. I like companies that nurture their talent," Dean said. "So, you must know this facility inside and out."

"Like the back of my hand," Marty beamed.

"Then you should understand that over half of your equipment is in the final twenty-five percent of its lifespan, and yet there were no budget items to put toward their replacement," Dean said.

"With the healthcare and regulatory changes, we have had our hands full, keeping our employees in place. I think once the dust is settled, we'll see the budget open up for those items," Marty stuttered.

"Production has decreased ten percent in the last five years, yet the total employee count for this plant has remained roughly static."

"Take care of the people, and the profits will come, Mr. Stevens says," Marty said exuberantly.

"That is an interesting business philosophy that I did not

encounter in grad school. By my calculations, the cost to replace the equipment, with a ten percent reduction in productivity and commensurate headcount would take over twenty years to pay off," Dean pressed.

Marty snapped his fingers, "Let me show you some of that equipment." Quickly leading Dean and Cassie into the heart of the production facility.

"This the Protogen 400. State of the art, thirty years ago. And yes, they have roughly a thirty-year lifespan on *average*. But look at this machine. Listen to it. The bearings are smooth, and there isn't a single seal that is leaking. The rep came out to give us a bid on replacement, and he told us to focus on other machines. It was in great shape."

Dean patted the steel casing, "Excellent, take care of your equipment, and it can reward you with a little bit of a grace period."

"And this beast," Marty walked Dean and Cassie to another hulking piece of equipment. "This machine did not fare so well. Despite impeccable maintenance, the pistons over time still failed, and the core gave out."

Dean looked confused, "Did you replace it? It seems to be running fine."

"Nope. Our chief mechanic and his team rebuilt it. Came in on a long weekend, tore it all apart and rebuilt with diesel engine parts. It has been running like a dream ever since," Marty beamed.

"I see. Talented mechanical team," Dean admitted, making a note in his binder.

"And that's not all, when North Site blew a rod through their primary turbine, our crew spent two weeks there to help get it up and running," Marty gloated.

"Teamwork, excellent. I like that."

"So," Marty rocked back and forth, looking hopefully at Dean.

"So…?" Dean frowned.

"What do you think? Worth keeping around, right?" Marty pandered.

Dean waved his hands, "I'm not here to evaluate cutting or retaining anything. Just getting a feel for what assets are in place, and what value each facility has now and in the foreseeable future."

"Well, let's get you in front of the real key assets here at the Holly Valley Site," Cassie suggested, winking at Marty, assuring him that he would take over from there.

Marty nodded and scampered back to his duties.

"Quite the hard sell," Dean whispered as they walked down the hall.

"It's more than the building, the machines, and the product. It's the people behind it. You saw the drive in. The people in an around this town? They rely on the Holly Vale site. It *is* the economy here," Cassie shared.

"I see. The crew have taken outstanding care of the production site," Dean replied.

"There is a lot of pride here. Anytime a family member goes to college, they know it was because of Cape Fear Commercial-Holly Vale. When someone buys a house, goes on vacation, retires, receives medical care...Holly Vale," Cassie said, looking directly at Dean.

"I get it. I get it. The site is important to the people and the town. So, noted."

Glancing at her watch, Cassie wrinkled her nose. "It is going to be tough to get up to North. You okay hanging with me for one more day?"

Dean closed his eyes and stood still for a moment. "Go up in the morning and be back in time for an afternoon meeting with Mr. Stevens?"

"Deal," Cassie held out her hand.

As Dean reached out to shake, Cassie pulled her hand back a bit. Dean looked at her questioningly.

"Just don't stand me up," Cassie laughed.

Dean rolled his eyes and sighed, "I won't."

"Sorry, couldn't resist," Cassie giggled. "Come on, let's get you back to your fancy car."

Chapter Seven -
Southern Charm

Dean lowered the top on the convertible as he waved goodbye to Cassie for the day. He was unhappy that Mr. Stevens drew the process out yet another day, but he felt better about how the day turned out given his history with Cassie. Dean had to admit that he had kind of enjoyed the tour.

As he drove back through the streets of Wilmington, the early evening sun was still warm on his skin. At a stoplight, he rolled up his sleeves. Looking at his shirt, he realized, he hadn't packed sufficient clothes for this long of a trip. In the hot and humid North Carolina business day, he needed another suit and shirt.

The idea of a suit being tailored in a short turn around was not reasonable. Dean decided to see what he could find as a reasonable solution. Punching in the shopping cue on the GPS, he followed it to a little row of shops between the beach and downtown. Pulling into a parking spot, his hopes were not high that he would walk away with a suit. Not one that would fit properly, anyway.

Seeing a store with quite well-attired mannequins in the front windows that bookended the entrance, Dean pushed his way inside.

A cheery woman looked up from her paperwork at the counter and greeted him.

Warily, Dean inquired, "I packed enough suit for two days, and by all accounts, I might be here all week. Any suggestions?"

"Well, it sounds like you have yourself quite the predicament," the lady eyed Dean, sizing him up. "Forty-two long with...low thirties waist."

Dean studied her for a moment, and then nodded, "That's right."

"Good luck finding anything off the shelf," the storekeeper laughed.

"I know."

"We do mostly custom here. Pick your swatch, and we'll make it perfect. Usually takes a few weeks though," the shopkeeper bit her lip. As she continued to measure Dean, she placed her hands on his shoulders and spun him around.

"Dean Taylor?" a voice called from a doorway leading to the back of the shop.

A well-dressed man burst through and strode up to Dean. "Shane Martin?" Dean called back.

"That's right," the man grinned, holding out his hand for Dean. "You remember Sarah?

Dean nodded in recognition, "Sarah West, the three of us did that Communications project together."

"Sarah Martin, now," Shane beamed.

"I see. That's fantastic," Dean admitted.

Sarah nodded, "We started dating right after we finished that project, and he just couldn't get rid of me."

Shane squeezed her shoulders close to his own, "Why would anyone want to get rid of you?" Kissing his wife on her head, he turned back to Dean.

"So, what brings you here?" Shane asked.

"I need some clothes," Dean admitted.

Shane laughed, "Not here. Here as in North Carolina."

Dean explained his work trip. "And it looks like my stay is extended a bit."

"Cape Fear Commercial has a great reputation, good people," Shane said. "It sounds like you could use another suit or two. A bit tough to put together in a short turn around. Let me see what we can do for you. We have a couple in the back that probably aren't too far off from your size. That customer isn't due back for two weeks. We can redo their order with a little extra elbow grease."

Disappearing into the back, Shane returned with two light-colored suits. "What do you think hon? A little nip and tuck?"

Sarah nodded, "I think that looks doable. We can probably have one done for you tomorrow, the other, maybe the next day?"

"You guys would do that for me?" Dean asked, incredulous.

"Sure, a fellow Seahawk, you bet," Shane said heartily.

"So, what about you? Find someone special in... Where did you move off to?" Sarah asked.

"California, and no," Dean admitted.

"Ah, it seemed like you were always on the hunt, for the right one, I mean," Sarah said, her face twisted in a knowing grin.

Dean shot his wife a quick look and then smiled, "Hey, we were just about to lock up. Love to have you over for dinner."

"I appreciate the offer. It would be nice, but I have to grab a few more things and get ready for my meetings tomorrow," Dean said.

"Sure, absolutely. Well, come on by tomorrow about this time, we'll have you fixed up," Shane said.

Dean thanked them and headed out of the shop. His mind was whirring as he left to return to his car. The warmth and hospitality of Shane and his wife were overwhelming.

Turning out of the clothing shop, he ran headlong into a woman saddled with two armloads of dry cleaning. As the two untangled themselves, they looked up at one another.

"I'm sorry, I...," Dean started, his hand placed against his chest to demonstrate his remorse. Once again, his hijacked brain rocked in recognition. His heart fell into the pit of his stomach with an acidic splash.

As the woman's own eyes flashed with acknowledgment, Dean's mind careened into a wild series of film clips. His arm around her shoulders as he walked her to class, consoling her after her boyfriend hurt her. Images of the two smiling across a flickering candle at a dinner table, leaving marks in the sand on moonlit beach walking hand in hand, cuddling at the tip of the bow of a ferry...turned into an argument over where their relationship was headed. Dean abruptly turned and left, leaving her college apartment, the door closing behind him, and their relationship ending at that very moment.

Dean closed his eyes momentarily, as the vision of her confronting him after that night met with blunt, cold, and utterly unmoving response from him. Tears running down her face, he nonchalantly turned and left. That was the last time they spoke. In that flash, he recalled the promises he had made to her, how he wouldn't treat her the way her previous boyfriend had, and there he was, likely doing worse. He got her to put her trust in him, and he let her down. Horrifically.

Sheepish and red-faced, Dean stammered, "Allie."

The woman wrinkled her nose, "Dean?"

"Yeah," he nodded. For a moment, taking Allie in, she was every bit as Dean remembered her, in all of the right ways. The shame of how he treated her overwhelmed him. His eyes dropped to the sidewalk, and he scuffed at it with his foot.

"It's good to see you," Allie smiled. "It's been, what? Nine…ten years?"

Dean nodded, "Ten years."

"Wow, you look great!" Allie acknowledged.

"So…so do you," Dean admitted softly. "Nice to see you. Are you good? I could help you with that stuff." He looked at the handful of garments, noting a suit and several men's dress shirts among the bundle.

Allie brightened, "No, I can handle it. But thank you."

"Okay," Dean swallowed hard. "Nice to see you."

Shuffling away quickly, Dean was overwhelmed with a feeling of awkwardness he had rarely encountered. Flustered, his face burned, and his stomach churned. Shaking his head, he sighed, "What a day."

Making a beeline for his rental car, he struggled to fish his keys out of his pocket.

"You know, you brought it on yourself," a voice called.

Dean's hand froze on the handle of the driver's door. "What?" Slowly, he spun to face the voice.

"That awkward feeling of running into people from the past. You created that feeling yourself in how you treated them and abruptly walked away," Allie said. Her voice was calm, matter-of-fact yet strangely friendly.

"I don't…I…," Dean began, and then his voice fell. Looking away for a moment, he collected himself. "I wanted to leave. I *had* to leave. Anything that remotely wrapped itself around me, that threatened to keep me here, I guess, I pushed them away."

Allie grimaced, "I'll say."

"I'm sorry."

"I know," Allie almost giggled as she responded. "You broke my heart, and I would guess a few others along the way, even your plutonic friends. People cared about you and you…you just turned and left them behind."

Dean looked confused, "Why does that seem to amuse you?"

Allie looked at Dean square in the eyes, "Because of how horrified you are to stand here and talk with me. Look, I'm not sure why you're back or for how long, but it's good to see you."

Allie turned and started for her minivan.

"A couple of days," Dean called. "I'm just here for a couple of days."

Allie nodded, opening her car door. As she turned to look at him once more, Dean added, "It was good to see you too."

Closing the door, Allie started the van and drove away. Dean sat behind the wheel of the Aston Martin, his finger hovering over the pulsing Start button. He felt sad, his stomach hurt, but he struggled to come to terms with exactly why. Dean hadn't led Allie or anyone on. He was truthful - a bit blunt, but honest. Yet, he felt as though he had committed a horrific thing. He was certain that he had.

The top-down drive back to the beach house and the welcoming chorus of waves released most of Dean's tensions from his run-ins. A weight still hung heavy in the further reaches of his mind. He had hoped the the open French doors with the surf pounding outside his balcony would sooth his eary soul. Dean flopped on the bed with a sigh.

Though his home in California was along the Pacific Coast, there was something different about the warmer waters and less populated beaches of the Carolinas. He remembered countless walks along those very beaches, whether under the guidance of the sun or the moon. With friends, girlfriends, his family, or just by himself, the Atlantic Ocean was a part of him. Like an old friend, it welcomed him.

Putting his past aside, he settled in for the night, ready to close the deal after the final site visit. He knew, with any luck, his trip down memory lane would be over by day's end.

Chapter Eight –
Extended Extension

Dean awoke with the same vigor as he had the previous day. Following a similar routine, he ran and swam before hitting the shower and getting dressed for the day.

Pulling on the same suit with a fresh shirt, he thought of Shane and Sarah and how nice to him they were the previous evening. Hoping that he might not, in fact, need those suits after all.

For a brief moment, his mind lit on Allie. The image in his head morphed from the innocent, bright-eyed girl that he helped through her broken relationship to the heartbroken, tear-stained face when he hurt her himself, to the easy-going unaffected woman he met last night. Shaking the entire card deck of images from his head, he focused on his day.

Dean fired up the Aston Martin and backed out of his

space. With a grin, he was determined to capitalize on the same skills that catapulted him to the top of Dana Holdings and make the long drive back to Charlotte to catch a flight home that evening.

Stopping on his way off of the island, as he had the morning before, Dean parked the convertible. Swinging the screen door wide, he was quickly greeted by a cheery voice. "You're back! I thought you'd be long gone to...Cali, right?"

Dean nodded, "Yes, California."

"Working the whole time? I was layin' at the beach after my shift yesterday. It was wonderful," the barista crooned.

"I did work a lot, but you know, I took a little time to hit the surf for a while," Dean admitted.

The girl's eyes widened, "You surf?" She eyed him for a moment, and scrunched her face, "You don't look the type."

Dean couldn't stifle a laugh, "You'd be surprised."

"Yeah, I guess," the barista nodded. "Let's see... cappuccino?"

"That'll be fine," Dean replied. "And a vanilla latte?"

The barista's eyes perked up, "Ooh, a lady friend. You work fast."

"Work associate," Dean corrected flatly.

"Right," the barista replied. "Here's your cappuccino. I'll have the latte right up."

Dean pulled in to the rear parking lot of the downtown Wilmington headquarters of Cape Fear Commercial. He sipped on his coffee until an SUV pulled in alongside him. Getting out, Dean walked over to the passenger door. Pulling on the handle, he found it locked.

"Are you going to let me in? I brought coffee," Dean offered, poking the latte through the open window.

Cassie smiled at him, "I like the coffee. You? I'm still considering."

Tilting his head, Dean frowned. Hearing a click, he opened the door.

"The coffee helps," Cassie assured him and slipped her SUV into gear.

"Have a nice evening?" Cassie asked.

Dean was thoughtful before replying, "It was fine, thanks."

Intuitively, Cassie pried, "What's up?"

"Nothing, it's...running into people I used to know. Did you know Shane and Sarah?"

"The Martin's? They're great. I see them every so often," Cassie nodded. Cocking her head briefly away from the road ahead of her, "You and Sarah...you didn't..."

"No!" Dean snapped. "We were friends, but no. Never."

"So, what's troubling you?"

Dean frowned, "Who says anything is troubling me?"

"We *did* date. I know that "fine" response means

something is wrong," Cassie pressed.

Sighing, Dean started to speak, wishing he could reel his words in as soon as they came out, "I ran into Allie Miller. I... I feel bad. I didn't... I didn't treat her as I wish I would have."

"Allie Miller," Cassie repeatedly thoughtfully. "She was your last girlfriend before you left town, as I recall."

"She was," Dean acknowledged.

"Nice girl."

"Yeah," Dean admitted.

"So...what about *that* one gets your goat?'

Dean closed his eyes for a moment before he spoke, "You remember her boyfriend, well, before me?"

"Mark?"

"Yeah."

"Kind of a piece of work, wasn't he? Prince who was actually very much a frog?" Cassie noted.

Dean nodded, "Yeah. He did a number on her. I was there."

"To pick up the pieces. The white knight and..."

"And then I wasn't," Dean admitted.

"And Dean Taylor officially has a conscience," Cassie beamed.

Rolling his eyes, Dean responded, "Of course I do."

"Did you feel bad about me?" Cassie asked coyly.

"Yes, I felt terrible. I just...I just had to...I'm sorry."

Cassie waved him off, "It's okay. We were young. Tell me, what makes Allie so different?"

"She trusted me. When she probably shouldn't have trusted any guy, she trusted me. And I let her down. Big time," Dean admitted.

Cassie reached across the console and patted him on the arm, "She's got over you just fine. She has a husband, two kids...I think she's okay."

"I know. I just..."

"It's what happens when you don't properly close doors. You take it all with you. You probably didn't even know you were carrying all that as you left and were enjoying your California life," Cassie noted.

Dean laughed, "It's funny. Driving in from Charlotte, as soon as I hit I-95, I was flooded with memories. A lot of good ones, but a lot of...guilt, too."

"You kind of brought that on yourself, Dean," Cassie noted.

Wrinkling his nose, Dean admitted, "That's what Allie said."

"Well, good talk, but we're here," Cassie said, pulling into the North facility.

Dean looked at his portfolio and breathed deeply, shaking off his personal life and focusing on getting the business deal closed.

"This is the plant that the Holly Vale crew came and fixed the primary turbine?" he asked.

"It is."

"How long ago was that?" he asked.

Cassie shrugged, "A couple of years."

"And they haven't looked at replacing it? Sounds like preventing a potential catastrophic failure would be a prudent measure," Dean mused.

"Well, you'll get to talk to Hank Stramm. He's the plant manager, about that yourself," Cassie said.

Nodding, Dean opened his door. Stretching his legs, he took in the facility. Like Holly Vale, the grounds were impeccable. The building itself, however, seemed to be showing its age. Making a note, he followed Cassie into the lobby of the building.

A well-weathered silver-haired man with a broad smile strode immediately to greet the two. Holding out a steady hand, he welcomed, "Hank Stramm, plant manager. Thank you for visiting."

"Hank, this is Dean Taylor. Don't be put off by his fancy California attire. He's North Carolinian by birthright," Cassie said.

"My family is from Brunswick County," Dean admitted. "I've been gone quite a while, though."

"Well, welcome back," Hank said. "So, what can we show you about our facility?"

Dean looked thoughtful, scanning his notes, he quickly

closed his portfolio, "This facility seems older than the others I have visited."

"It is. North Side was retrofitted for Cape Fear Commercial almost twenty years ago. Used to be a textile facility making upholstery for the furniture makers in Hickory. Bart heard it was for sale, inspected the equipment, and decided we could use the floor plan and some of the machines for our ancillary line. Some of that original equipment is still up and running," Hank beamed.

Dean's concern was unveiled in a slight frown, "It's that original equipment that has me concerned, such as your primary turbine?"

Hank nodded, "Marty shared that with you, huh? Pretty good act of company teamwork. We're kind of a big family at Cape Fear. She's up and running, probably as smooth as she ever has been."

"And the other equipment?" Dean pressed.

"There are a few pieces that are showing their teeth, but we keep production on schedule," Hank admitted.

Dean paused in stride, his eyes thoughtfully looking past the plant manager to the products of various stages of manufacture. "And this is all for ancillary product lines, not intrinsic to the Cape Fear brand?"

Hank shot Cassie a look and began to speak before she stepped in, "The canvas line has developed a strong following in the yachting community from sails to covers."

Flipping through his pack of data, Dean noted, "But from a profit and loss standpoint, it's never achieved better than treading water."

"Yes, but the collateral impact on the rest of the company's products makes North Side pull its weight from an overall corporate perspective," Cassie countered.

Dean's face fell flat as he tried to reconcile her statement with his analysis. His expression did not allow either Cassie or Hank a vibe on whether it left him with a positive or negative view of the facility.

Hank's eyes kept begging Cassie to steer the conversation to the viability of North Side and the issues requiring her public relations skillset over his operations experience.

Slipping her arm inside Dean's, she tugged him gently, "Come on. Let me show you the heart and soul of North Side."

Exiting out of the rear of the plant, past the machines and the loading bay and the people making them run, they found themselves on a trail that followed along a creek.

Raising an eyebrow, Dean asked, "This is nice and all, but what does this have to do with the North Side plant?"

"You'll see," Cassie grinned, giving his arm a slight squeeze.

Dean quietly admitted to himself that the short walk along the trail was pleasant. The winding path mirrored the creek as it snaked away from the factory. The sun bounced its way through the green canopy that shaded either side of the stream. He even enjoyed being close to Cassie, remembering what drew them together as friends in the first place. Dean had nearly gotten over the discomfort of facing his past with Cassie, and how he left things- how he hurt her.

It wasn't long before the trail left the forest for the small town of North Side. Dean wasn't sure it might have been even smaller and more quaint than Holly Vale from the day before.

"Okay. Another cute town, another heartbreaking story about the factory if closed would send a ripple effect through the community," Dean said, his eyes casting a presumptive gaze.

Cassie studied Dean's eyes for a moment, "Actually, North Side has an even more direct connection to the facility. When the upholstery company set to close and Bart caught wind of it, he came up to check it out. Like you, he had reservations about its usefulness from a production standpoint and whether Cape Fear needed its particular type of output."

"So why did he go through with it? It seems like a distraction and burden to the company and its bottom line," Dean assessed.

"Because he knew the town would die without it," Cassie said, her voice serious.

Dean laughed, "Oh, come on. That's a bit dramatic."

"No. While Holly Vale certainly thrives from our facility there, North Side is in existence because Cape Fear Commercial,"

Cassie stressed. "You saw the drive in. There is not a lot of industry, source of jobs for people for miles. Mr. Stevens saw how this community worked together, lived together. He saw that heart and soul as a powerful addition to Cape Fear."

"And saved a town in the process," Dean added.

"Precisely," Cassie grinned.

"Mr. Stevens has an interesting perspective on running a business. I am not sure the folks on Wall Street would necessarily subscribe to his methodologies," Dean said.

Cassie shot him a look, "Are we worried about Wall Street or Orange County?"

"I can't say as though Dana Holdings will agree with *all* of Mr. Stevens' decisions," Dean admitted.

"The question for today, as our advocate, as the advocate for the people of Holly Vale and North Side…and Wilmington does Dean Taylor agree?"

Dean was quiet as his eyes reviewed the town before falling back onto Cassie, "I'll see if I can't make the case for collateral benefit to the rest of the organization. Think you can get me as much data as you can to help tell that story?"

Cassie squeezed his arm tight as she smiled up at him, "I'll get the accounting team to put something together."

"Let's get back and close this thing," Dean said softly, "I can tell you most companies would shutter it. Anyone else at Dana Holdings would, I know that."

"Mr. Stevens will have his team assembled, as promised, this afternoon. In the meantime, it *is* lunchtime. Let's complete the tour of North Side with a visit to Jan's bakeshop. She makes the best pot pie," Cassie suggested.

Dean nodded, "I could eat."

As they settled into their seats at the small restaurant, the smell of sweet and savory baked goods overwhelmed him. Dean smiled, "How can a smell make your stomach growl so much?"

"Right? It's wonderful," Cassie took in a deep breath to enjoy the scent and accentuate the point. Snapping her gaze to Dean, she teased, "Do they eat carbs in California?"

"Are there carbs in tofu?" Dean volleyed.

"Eww, you don't really eat that stuff, do you?"

Dean laughed, "No. I don't."

"I'm glad it was you they sent," Cassie said, looking at Dean.

"You know, so am I," Dean admitted. "Thank you for making the past few days…pleasant. It could have been bizarre."

Cassie wore a confused expression on her face, "You mean it hasn't been weird?"

"Well, it has been, just not *really* weird," Dean laughed.

Aa sing-song voice calling out Cassie's name sidelined the conversation.

"Hi Jan," Cassie waved as a bubbly woman, who reminded

Dean a bit of Mrs. Claus, sauntered to the table.

"And who is the handsome gentleman?" the woman asked, her eyebrows raised.

Cassie giggled, "Handsome, perhaps. Gentleman…"

"I'm Dean Taylor, ma'am."

"Ooh, manners. I believe a gentleman, to be sure," the joyful lady sang. "My name is Jan Evers, the best baker within fifty miles of North Side. To be fair, I am the only baker within fifty miles of North Side."

"If your food tastes as good as it smells, I'd pen you in for best on the eastern seaboard," Dean offered.

Jan feigned amazement, "And charming, too."

"He is in town touring our facilities," Cassie said. "He is an old…friend."

"I see," Jan tilted her head knowingly. "What is the word on the old beast? Without that sentinel, well, North Side flat out wouldn't be here."

"That is the message I have received. I'll see what I can do to impress its vitality and how amazing the people are here. The quality of food and service, clearly serve high marks for the marketplace," Dean assured.

As Jan walked away with their lunch orders, Cassie leaned forward, "It's that charm that got me in trouble the first time."

Dean cocked his head, "First time?"

Cassie shook herself, "I mean at *all*."

Smiling, Dean offered, "It's okay. I enjoy your friendship. I wouldn't want to mess that up *this* time."

Cassie looked relieved as she studied his eyes, "Good. Me too, *friend.*"

Chapter Nine –
To Sign or Not to Sign

Dean was confident as he followed Cassie into the historic Wilmington home-turned-office. Charlotte followed with a pitcher of iced tea and another of water as they took their seats around the conference table.

Setting his lucky pen alongside the contract, Dean sat up straight and folded his hands on top of the papers as he waited. With a deep breath, he transformed into his game face – serious, poised, yet affable.

Cassie quietly observed his mannerisms behind her glass of iced tea.

Chester and Jacob were once again the first to arrive. Like they had the previous meeting, they both sat down across from Dean with a chair left between them. This time, Bart Stevens entered only moments later.

With a broad smile, the Cape Fear Commercial CEO said, "I trust your visits have been well?"

Dean paused before he spoke, "They have. I am most impressed, as I am sure was your and Ms. Sutton's intention, with the people. At all sites, they work well together, tackling challenges for the benefit of the organization. I like that."

"I see," Stevens looked pleased. "I am glad to hear that. Taking the people into account is first and foremost on my list to proceed."

"Great, with that, I think it is time we move forward," Dean spun the contract to face Mr. Stevens and held the pen out.

To Dean's dismay, the CEO did not move an inch at the gesture.

"I appreciate your time out there with Cassie and your candor," Stevens said, cocking his head to one side, "I believe your words, as well. I am wary that your executive team won't necessarily heed them."

"Sir, if I may, I have full faith in Dean's sincerity. He genuinely sees the value and the necessity of maintaining the sites and the people. All of them," Cassie interjected.

"It's true. And you are not wrong for being concerned. Most corporations might not value what each site brings, the scale of the operation or the structure of the current levels of staffing," Dean conceded. "From an intrinsic fiduciary value, there are some flaws. A few are quite serious. But in working with Ms. Sutton and spending time at your sites, I can make a case that the individual pieces, even those struggling to stand on their own, in aggregate yield a higher return and perform better together."

Mr. Stevens smiled, nodding at the youthful negotiator, "I like how you think. That is a good way to push for retention. I do believe that is the recommendation to push forward to your executive team."

The CEO pushed back from the table and leaned back in his seat, "The challenge I have is that time and distance have a way of diluting and changing perspective. Especially as your time on the project ends and your actuaries and continuity managers take it over for you. No, I am just not satisfied that this is a lasting equation. I can't risk my employees, their families, those towns...I just can't."

The room fell silent for several minutes. Dean struggled to find a visual point to focus on instead of the people in the room. He maintained his aloof composure and ultimately allowed his eyes to follow on the series of old photos on the wall behind Mr. Stevens.

As the impasse continued, Dean would typically have risen from his chair and started his walk toward the door. This case was different. The stakes for him and his career were too significant. The stakes for the towns and the employees of Cape Fear Commercial were too high. He didn't want to let Cassie down.

Mr. Stevens broke the silence, his eyes raised, and his face brightened and offered a wry smile, "I've got it. Tell you what, I'll sign *right now* if you want to relocate and run this division for Dana Holdings yourself."

Dean was shocked at the suggestion. Gauging by the stunned expressions of Chester and Jacob, they were too. Shooting a glance at Cassie, Dean formulated his response.

Hands waving in front of him, he politely declined, "Sir, I appreciate your confidence and faith in me. I have commitments in California. I have a life there. I can find someone that can meld your organization, all of it intact, guaranteed that…"

Stevens shook his head, "No, no…too easy to ride that wave for a while, and then a bad quarter and severance package later, the people who are part of the Cape Fear culture are victims of a corporate change of heart."

Typically unflappable, Dean caught himself breathing in a deep, audible sigh. "Sir, what do you suggest? How do we proceed?"

"Man of action, I like that," Stevens beamed. "I'd like you to complete your tour of the facilities. Gather what information you need from accounting, operations, sales…everything, myself included, are at your disposal."

"And then we can sign?"

"And then we have our annual company picnic this weekend. I'd like you to attend as my guest. And then we can discuss signing," the CEO countered.

In the corner of his eye, he could see Cassie giggle to herself at what must have been his outward expression of the startled, choking response that he felt.

"This weekend?" Dean stressed, clicking off the days on his mental calendar to get to that point.

"Sure," Stevens shrugged. "You've seen the plants, met the employees, toured their towns. I'd like you to visit the families, the children behind the workers and those towns. *Then*, we can see what kind of clauses, guarantees, and verbiage you can bake into the contract. We can see what personal investment you can pack with you as you head back to California with my company in your hands."

Once more, the room fell ghostly silent. Dean's mental score ran up a dominating tally for the businessman with whom he had been sparring. He had to admit, he was impressed. He had owned rooms of Fortune 500 executives and pulled every string in the negotiation. This lighthearted, easy-going southern gentleman was indeed shrewd.

Not seeing another avenue to proceed, Dean relented, "Very well. I'll write up a request for everything I will need to present the case that secures each location, especially North Side."

"I'll have Charlotte send you the details on the company picnic. We'll enjoy having you," Mr. Stevens said. His voice never faltered from his affable tone. "Cassie, will you see to it that Mr. Taylor has everything else that he needs? Access to meeting rooms, team leaders, heck, the lunchroom."

"Of course, sir," Cassie nodded.

"There we have it," Mr. Stevens said, getting up and reaching a hand across the table, "It's a pleasure to work with you."

Dean shook his hand, and the CEO, along with his quiet entourage of left and right hand, left the room.

Cassie smiled quietly over the top of her iced tea glass.

Dean turned his attention to her, "Yes?"

"Ever have negotiations like this one in California?"

Dean winced, "Not in L.A., Chicago or New York."

"He is a good man. *Way* more astute than most would give him credit for at first glance. I attest it is the loving way he manages this company. He rejects unnecessary compromises in a way a father would refute any attempt to tear his family apart," Cassie said.

"It is effective, whatever the reasoning," Dean admitted. "So, I guess you are still on as my tour guide?"

"Something like that. I don't really have much public relations work to do while we are in negotiation. My plate is relatively clear outside of helping prep for the company picnic," Cassie said. Glancing at her watch, she added, "In fact, I need to be off to attend the final planning meeting. Leave a list with Charlotte with anything you need or…here is my card. It has my cell on it if you need me for anything."

Dean accepted the card, "Thank you. It has been an

unexpectedly pleasant week."

A crooked grin swept across Cassie's lips, "The week has only just begun, and it looks like you are in for longer, wilder ride than anticipated."

"Thank you for sticking up for me," Dean said.

"Don't let me down," Cassie said adding sharply, "*Again.*"

Dean watched her get up and leave for her meeting, her words stinging just a bit. He sat for several moments in the conference room by himself. While he had the path forward, or so he thought, he was still trying to determine how the deal that he thought would be an easy one to close had unraveled to be so complicated.

He was snapped out of his thoughts by a voice from the doorway, "Is everything okay, Mr. Taylor?"

"Charlotte...yes. I'm fine. I was just collecting my thoughts," Dean replied.

"Mr. Taylor is quite the businessman," the receptionist said.

Dean laughed, "You have no idea."

As Dean started down the tight roads of Downtown Wilmington, he figured he might as well respond to the countless emails, texts, and phone calls from his boss demanding an update.

Filling his boss in on the day's events and especially the meeting Bart Stevens, Dean allowed the slower traffic to keep the wind noise of the convertible down for his conversation.

"Whooo," Marshall called in to the phone after listening to Dean's recap. "I thought you had this thing dialed, 'I'll have this closed out in forty-eight hours,' I believe you said. You sure you're okay out there? Playing in front of the old hometown crowd giving you the yips? Taking you off your game a bit?"

"No, sir. Just playing a little hardball… Well, more like softball. He was pulling heartstrings all that kind of stuff. Wanting guarantees on keeping current staff and facilities intact," Dean reported.

"You know we can't guarantee things like that. Come up with some language that suggests we can, and we will. Insert some clauses that sound nice, but we know they have no real teeth to them," Marshall commanded. "Just get it signed. We'll see in a few quarters how much consolidation and restructuring we'll have to do."

"Yes, sir."

"I have faith in you, Dean," Marshall said before cutting off the call.

Approaching the more open roads toward the beach, he was happy to end the conversation and allow the convertible's growl, mixed with the rushing wind to free his mind. This case was taking a toll on him, and he knew his promotion to partner was riding on its successful completion.

Chapter Ten –
The Run In

Taking his frustrations out on the surf, Dean rose from the frothy breakwater a new man. After several runs, he headed back to the house with energy in his step. Regardless of which coast he was on, he was glad to have the power of the ocean's guidance towards an improved perception.

Cleaning off the salt and sand, he realized his toiletries and essential clothing had quickly depleted. Checking his watch, he realized that he should be off to retrieve his suit from Shane and Sarah.

Firing up the convertible, he drove the short distance to the clothing shop. Arriving just before closing, he pushed through the front door, a light chime announcing his presence.

"There he is," Shane called with gusto. "Honey, Dean's here. You mind grabbing the suit from back there?"

"Thank you again for doing this. You guys are life savers," Dean said.

Shane brushed him off, "Aww, you'd do the same in reverse. That's what friends, old or new, are all about."

Dean nodded, wondering if, in his heart, he knew that to be true.

"This is going to look great on you," Sarah said, holding the suit up. "You want to try it on? Make sure we made the adjustments right for you?"

Dean accepted the suit, "No, I have all the faith that you nailed it."

"Hey, we're just about to close up. How about it? Have dinner with us?" Shane proposed.

"Yeah," Sarah nodded. "We'd love to have you."

Dean hesitated for a moment. The couple was infectious. He felt genuinely uplifted being with them, yet he felt oddly like an imposter accepting their generosity.

"I would love to," he declined politely, "This negotiation has been more challenging than I had predicted. I'll be burning the midnight oil as it is. Thank you, though."

Shane laughed, "You were always the driven one. Gosh, it's great to see you."

"The invitation is open. Just let us know so we can set a spot at the table," Sarah said handing him the store's business card, "Our cell numbers are on there. You are welcome anytime."

"Thank you. You two are...wonderful," Dean said.

"Well, good luck. Let us know if there is anything we can do to help," Shane offered.

Dean nodded and walked out with his new suit. As he walked to the sports car, he wondered if he would ever be in a relationship like theirs. If he could ever be mature enough to be that gracious.

Pressing the start button on the Aston Martin, he suddenly felt like a pretentious shell of himself. He struggled to put a pin on who he really was. He thought he was a good person. He thought he tried to do the right things, but watching how people like Shane and Sarah interacted, he wasn't so sure he stacked up. When he thought about the people he had run into on his visit from his past, he was suddenly very clear about himself. He absolutely did not stack up.

Sighing, he pulled out of the clothing shop parking lot and put the nearest grocery store into his GPS so that he could stock up on basics for the rest of the week.

Laden with a basket full of essential toiletries for a somewhat more extended stay than he had planned, Dean made his way to the checkout stand. A woman in front of him tried to steer her children away from the candy placed at their eye levels while at that same time unload her cart.

He danced around for a moment, wishing he had arrived in front of her so that he did not have to wait. Instead, he waited awkwardly behind the mild chaos.

Dean took a closer look as she turned to pull her youngest away from the candy shelf and pointed in the direction of their cart. He recognized her as his waitress from the restaurant on the pier. For a moment, it looked like he had caught her eye as well and was about to say 'hello' when she immediately diverted her eyes and swiveled her hips so that should could avoid direct eye contact.

By the time she had her children in order and placed the last item from her very full cart onto the belt, the cashier was finished and patiently waited for her to pay. Scrambling in her purse, she ultimately placed it down on the counter so that she could rifle through it with both hands. Sighing, she looked out the grocery store windows.

Embarrassed, her cheeks increasingly growing increasingly crimson, she said, "I'm sorry. I can't find my wallet. I must have left it at home."

Before the cashier could reply, the waitress snapped her fingers, "I pulled it out to pay bills. It's sitting on the kitchen table. I suppose that revelation doesn't really help, does it?"

"Ma'am, I can cancel the transaction. You can always come back. I can try to hold back the non-frozen items for you, if you like," the cashier said. Looking at the cookie crumbs on the youngest child's shirt. "And we can just forget about the cookies."

The exasperated woman looked at the cashier, then her

children, and whispered hoarsely, "I'm sorry."

Dean raised his hand, partway, "Maybe I can help. It's...Shelby, right? From the restaurant. Here, let me pay. I really don't mind."

Shelby's jaw dropped slightly at the offer and then tightened, "No, thank you. I can't have you do that. I'll just come back."

"It's no big deal. I am sure you and your kids, who appear to be a ton of fun, would rather not make two trips to the grocery store tonight," Dean stated.

Looking down at her children who stared back with wide, hopeful eyes, she breathed out a deep sigh and relented, "Okay, but on one condition. I get to make it up to you and pay you back. Come by the restaurant tomorrow night. It'll be my treat."

"Deal," Dean smiled. "I'll just have my stuff added to the sale and take care of it. You guys have a nice night."

Shelby stared at him for a long moment. Reluctantly, her cheeks still sporting a healthy shade of red, she replied curtly, "Thank you."

Without another word or a look backward, she spun and pushed her cart with her kids in tow out of the grocery store, leaving Dean to add his items and complete the transaction.

"Mommy, who was that man?" the oldest of the two children asked.

"No one, honey. Just a man at the grocery store."

Dean slid his credit card into the slot and grabbed his bags of groceries. He paused on the way to his car as Shelby was putting the final bit of groceries in her well-worn vehicle.

He readied a wave, but she refused eye contact. Moving her body in a concerted, yet odd fashion, she climbed into her driver's seat. Checking her children's seatbelts, she started the old car and pulled away in the opposite direction of Dean and his convertible.

Shrugging, he climbed into his own driver's seat and brought the sports car to life. With a flip of a switch and press on the throttle, he rocketed back towards the beach house.

The setting sun cast a myriad of pink, orange, and red highlights on the few wispy clouds that hung over the Atlantic Ocean. Dean sorted through the events and the people that made up his day. Working with Cassie had been far more enjoyable than he thought while closing the deal, not the easy path to success he expected as he flew across the country.

Shane and Sarah had affected him, too with their relationship as a couple and how kind they were to him. He tried to reconcile why the positive experience made him feel bad.

Then there was Shelby, the waitress. He had no idea why he interjected. He purposely avoided paying attention to people at the store when he was at home. Why he not only noticed but interceded tonight, he did not know.

"This whole town is making me crazy," he mumbled to

himself as he shook any thought out of his head that didn't have to do with the open-air sports car or taking a dip in the Atlantic Ocean.

Chapter 11 -
Something to Work With

Dean woke with a fire in his stomach. He was excited to get to work and make progress on the final package. Ensuring he was of a clear mind, he followed the same routine that he had for most of the week- a run, a swim, and a stop by the coffee shop.

"Back yet again. My witty banter hasn't chased you off yet?" the barista smiled from behind the counter.

"I don't know. Maybe I'm just not awake enough for it to resonate," Dean quipped.

"Ha, good one," the barista laughed. "Hey, I have something for you."

Dean cocked his head, curious what a barista at a coffee shop would have for him.

"Ta-da!" she sang as she raised a bottle for him to see. "I ordered almond milk. I think you asked for it the first time you came in."

"I did," Dean acknowledged. "Thank you. An almond milk latte it is."

"Just the one?"

"Make a vanilla latte, if you will, for me," Dean added. "What's your name, by the way?"

The girl stopped what she was doing and tilted her head, "I'm Olivia."

"Olivia, it's nice to meet you. I'm Dean."

"So, Dean, it seems you're with us a little longer than you thought. Is that a good thing?"

Dean shrugged, a wry smile crossing his lips, "Hasn't been all that bad of a thing."

"Right on," Olivia flashed a smile. "I'll get your drinks for you."

The screen door squealed, announcing additional customers. Instinctively, Dean turned. A young man and his family filtered in behind him in line. They were well prepared for a day at the beach. The man had a Semper Fi tattoo on his forearm.

As Olivia bounced back to the counter with Dean's drinks, he handed over two large bills. Olivia frowned at the amount.

"Use that what for whatever they want," Dean instructed.

"Uhm, this will be way more than enough," Olivia protested.

"Probably," Dean nodded.

"What do I do with it?"

"Whatever you would like. It's yours," Dean said. "Have a great day, Olivia. Thank you for the almond milk."

Nodding at the man standing with his family, Dean called on his way out, "Thank you for your service."

Dean arrived at the Cape Fear Commercial office building just as Cassie was pulling in. Leaning out of her driver's side window, she said, "That is a beautiful car. I'm not going to lie."

Seeing Dean once again with a cup of coffee, she smiled, "You should start bringing one for Bart, not me. He's the one making the decision."

"So, noted," Dean turned away from Cassie's SUV and started toward the office. "I'll just bring this to him."

Cassie reached out and softly tapped his arm, "Well, I am one of his closest advisors."

Handing her the coffee cup, he asked, "What's the plan for today?"

"There is a massive amount of data being compiled and sent to your email inbox as we speak. It's really up to you. What will help you put your case together?"

"Who are your primary customers for the products produced at North Side?" Dean asked.

Cassie shrugged, "We sell through distributors all over the

globe, along with some custom work." Snapping her fingers, she brightened, "I know just where I am taking you."

"Okay. Let's go," Dean started walking towards the passenger seat of Cassie's SUV.

Remaining where she was, she called, "Where we're going, I think your car will do just fine."

Dean smiled, giving his keys a light toss in the air, "Alright."

Opening the door, he let Cassie into the passenger seat and glided over to the driver's seat. As he brought the convertible down the road, he glanced at his passenger. She sipped on her coffee, a pleasant look on her face beneath her sunglasses, seemingly taking in every moment of the open-air car ride towards the coast.

"Head toward the Wrightsville Beach Marina, I'll guide you once we get there," Cassie said with her head pushed back in the luxury seat.

Following her instructions, Dean quickly navigated the easy Wilmington roads to close in on the marina. He nearly had to nudge her to snap her out of her summertime daze when they arrived.

"Head down to the building at the dry docks. We'll duck in there for a bit to see our products ready for install. Then we can head down to the docks and see them in action," Cassie directed.

"Sounds good," Dean nodded, holding his hand out for her to take the lead.

Cassie poked through the giant bay doors of the marina. On either side of a full path that a variety of vehicles used to move boats and parts were large racks storing boats in neat rows, stacked three high.

At one end of the bay was a maintenance area where mechanics worked on engines. Detailers brought boats to a shine, and installers dressed boats with new accessories. Cassie led Dean to a man who was busy stringing a canvas Bimini top over the pilot station and stern of a vessel.

"Cape Fear Commercial?" Cassie called up to the man working on the canvas as he reached for another tool.

The man paused and studied the two for a moment, "Yep."

"We're with Cape Fear, I'm introducing to my friend, Dean, why folks like you choose to buy from us," Cassie said.

The man shrugged, "Could use any vendor for this work, I suppose. Cape Fear is good craftsmanship. I use most of their other accessories, so I like the fact that I can get tops like this custom, and they fit right into place. Besides, they're the home team. If I was in Florida or California...I don't know."

"Thanks," Dean nodded. "The boat looks great."

Cassie and Dean walked through the rest of the dry dock building. She would point out other installs or Cape Fear Commercial parts as they passed. Finding their way to the marina docks, they strolled along the water, occasionally admiring a boat or taking notice of the accessories adorned.

"Could use any vendor, not a resounding statement for North Side, huh?" Cassie admitted.

Dean shrugged, understanding the potential impact of the statement, "It's not great on the surface. There were some good points that we could capitalize on, though. No-fuss fit using Cape Fear canvas with Cape Fear accessories."

Cassie laughed, "A good point for a PR director to pick up on, huh?"

"It could be the final decision-making straw for someone working on a boat in Seattle or the Bahamas. Could help sell either product," Dean said.

"Mr. Stevens demands... can you pull them off?" Cassie asked as they strolled down the docks.

Dean paused. Looking past Cassie and at the sun playing on the water, he replied, "I'm the best chance he has unless we can find another Mr. Stevens out there wanting to invest like he did so many years ago. Someone with a bigger heart for people than their wallet. That is not exactly the venture capital and acquisition mindset. Numbers and numbers only rule the game."

"Then why are you still here? I would think most negotiators would have walked out by now," Cassie asked.

"That was my instinct," Dean admitted. "I have a lot riding on this sale. Aa partner role in the firm is waiting for me as soon as I get the contract in hand."

"I see," Cassie's voice fell flat. Slowly she continued their stroll down the dock and her interest in the boats diminished.

"I didn't want to tour the plants. I had no interest in what the plant managers had to say or the bleeding heart reasons to keep a facility running when it, from a pure business case decision, should be shuttered," Dean confessed. "But it was good that Mr. Stevens made me. It was good that you showed me the perspective beyond the building, beyond the products. It left an impression on me."

Cassie stopped again and looked directly into Dean's eyes, "So..."

"So, I promise, I will do what I can," Dean said.

"I'm trusting you," Cassie said, her voice stern.

Dean nodded, his eyes absorbing the scene along the harbor. He hoped his days of broken promises were behind him.

Chapter Twelve - Too Many Exes

Dean followed up his day with Cassie by attacking the late afternoon shore break. The sets built nicely, allowing for some of the best surfing he'd enjoyed since his return to Carolina beaches.

No matter how busy and stressful his days were, how full and burdened his mind might get, a visit to the beach and succumbing to the power of the ocean cleared his mental slate and brought him to a satiated state of Zen.

He didn't know how many waves he rode to shore, but when the sun began to melt beyond the mainline, he allowed the Atlantic to carry him home one final time. As he marched up the sand towards the beach house, he remembered the offer from the waitress at the grocery store.

Realizing he had salted away most of the evening, he hurried to get cleaned up.

As the doors to the restaurant were pulled open, Dean strode through. He was met by the hostess, who asked where he would like to sit.

Hesitating, he shuffled awkwardly, "In Shelby's section?"

The response caught the hostess by surprise. Tilting her head, she eyed Dean from head to toe before a wry smile pursed her lips, "Alright."

Dean followed the hostess out to the first set of tables along the pier, closest to the dining room. As the hostess passed Shelby, she gave a little wink, which was met by a disapproving scowl from the waitress.

As he settled into his seat, he had scarcely a moment to enjoy the beach scene before a southern voice gathered his attention, "I didn't think you were going to come."

"Sorry to come so late," Dean apologized, "After work, I decided to hit the waves for a bit."

"Oh, you're a *surfer*," Shelby acknowledged, with a slight roll of her eyes.

Dean cocked his head and wrinkled his nose, "Is that a bad thing?"

"Not necessarily a good thing," Shelby intoned flatly. "I'll be right back with water and your money."

Before Dean could speak, the waitress whisked away.

In moments, she returned with a pitcher of water. After

filling his glass, she dipped into her waist apron and pulled out a wad of dollars.

"Here you go. Thank you," Shelby said, her voice devoid of emotion. "Dinners on me."

"You really don't have to, I don't mind…," Dean started.

Shelby visibly tensed, "I don't need a white knight riding in to save my day. I can take care of myself. I don't need guests thinking more of my witty repartee than I am merely serving them food, trying to get through my shift so that I can go home and be with my children."

Dean stared quietly at the waitress, lost in what to say, or what brought on her reaction.

Softening, she admitted, "Look, all week long, especially during tourist season, there are men who come in here on vacation, a work trip, fishing with the boys who see me getting paid to be nice to them, thinking they can whisk me away from my poor Cinderella life."

"Okay…," Dean said empathetically, not fully understanding what the tirade to do with him.

"I'm sorry. I don't mean to unleash on you. I'm not even sure why I did that," Shelby confessed. With a big sigh, she asked, "What can I get for you?"

"It's late. What's the easiest thing for the kitchen to make?" Dean asked.

"A to-go box," Shelby spat, once more in an even

emotionless voice.

"That was a joke," Dean said slowly.

"Yes, it was." Shelby's stoic face slid just for a moment into a cracked smile. "The kitchen stays open for the bar menu. It's okay. They'll make whatever you want."

"If I'm your last table, why don't I move to the bar? They have outside tables, it's the same to me," Dean offered. A look of protest washed over Shelby's face. Dean laughed, "It is okay, I don't mind. You can even join me, in the full safety of your co-workers, for a bite if you still need to eat."

Shelby shook her head as she stammered, "I... I don't... I'll think about it."

Dean grabbed his water glass and stood up. Shelby stared at him briefly, before consenting and returning to her duties to close out her shift.

Settling into his new table, he placed his order with the bar waitress and stared out at the beach lit by the lights of the pier. He enjoyed watching the ribbons of white well up seemingly out of nowhere before being highlighted by the lights. The ocean seemed to stretch forever under the starry sky.

A light touch on his shoulder broke his attention. Turning, he was surprised to see Allie with a couple of other women at her heels. "Dean!"

Standing up from his chair, he smiled a hello.

"Ladies, this is Dean Taylor, high school crush," Allie

introduced. "Dean, this is Morgan and Sue. It's Sue's birthday, so I have trusted the kids to my husband for a couple of hours."

"Nice to meet you, Happy Birthday, Sue," Dean said. "Good to see you again, Allie."

"You too," Allie beamed.

As Allie leaned in to hug Dean, he caught Shelby in the corner of his eye as she made her way into the bar. "He's a bit of a heartbreaker. I have to confess," Allie teased.

Dean fell contrite at the comment, looking past Allie's shoulder, Shelby had disappeared.

"Well, I don't want to keep you from your dinner, and the girls and I have a narrow window before returning to the home front. Good to see you, Dean," Allie said cheerily and moved further down the deck overhanging the beach to their table.

Dean stared for a moment at the spot he had spied Shelby, but she was gone.

Resigned to his fate of dining solo, he leaned back to absorb the evening at the beach. His mind tugged away from the crashing waves. He mindlessly ordered his meal as Allie's words resonated. She was kind and welcoming to him, but he couldn't fight the images of the last days they were together, how he'd treated her. The photos in his head made his stomach churn.

The scene, a decade old, replayed in his head. He left her in a lurch, and he knew it. He cared about her. He knew that, but he shed her like an itchy sweater on a hot summer's day. Driven to peel away from her, divorce himself of the last Carolina connection that he had, no matter the cost. The cost he had run away from without a moment's look over his shoulder. Allie was a sweet, young woman who deserved way better than what he had delivered.

He sank in his seat, pushing away his plate and instead reaching for the bourbon he ordered in place of his glass of wine. Over the rim of the glass, he caught Allie laughing and enjoying her time with her friends. He was grateful that she had a good life for herself, and the selfish interactions of men like him hadn't deterred from that.

What he struggled with was all of the people from his past that were so kind to him. He couldn't understand why, when on his way out of town, he pushed his way through all of them to get to his exit and didn't take a single glance back. Now here he was, not of his own accord, back in Carolina, the recipient of so much underserved, unrequited kindness.

His life and his role in other people's lives came crashing down on him. Absentmindedly, he shook his head at himself, finishing the bourbon in a single, final gulp. Pushing away from the table, he took a subtle glance at Allie. Closing his eyes briefly, he winced at the pain that he had caused her and was now absorbing himself.

Walking out of the restaurant, he lowered the top on the convertible. The car elicited a bellowing complaint from its exhaust as Dean took his frustration and motivation out on the pedal, pressing the accelerator hard.

Chapter Thirteen – An Apology Tour

Dean forewent his beach routine as he wanted to jump right into his analysis to draw up the final clauses for the contract. One part of the routine he elected not to forego was a quick trip to the coffee shop.

Wheeling into a parking spot right in front of the shop, he climbed out and swung open the screen door. "Good morning, Olivia!" he called as he stepped in out of the brilliant morning light.

"Surfer, businessman Dean," the barista beamed. "Uh, I have something for you."

Dean looked surprised, "What? The almond milk was a great treat. What do you have for me today?"

For the first time since he visited the coffee shop, Olivia was subdued, "The extra money from yesterday, it was too much."

Dean shrugged, "You caught me with a gesture of kindness

on a day when I needed it. Thinking of him, even just as a silly customer passing through, was appreciated. Use it for school, a new surfboard, or save it for customers who come in and really need it."

"You're not going to take it back, are you?"

Dean smiled, "Nope."

"Fine!" Olivia grumbled. "The two lattes today?"

"My coworker will have to fend for herself. Just mine this morning," Dean replied. The squeak of the screen door announced another visitor. Reflexively, Dean turned to see an older man with a veteran's ball cap on his head. "And whatever that gentleman would like."

Overhearing, the man stopped, surprised. As he started to wave off the gesture, Dean cut him off. "Already a done deal, I insist."

Relenting, the man put his hands down and gave Olivia his order.

Grabbing his cup, Dean turned to leave. "Thank you for your service, sir." Reaching out, Dean gave the man a handshake.

Shelby stood in the shadow of the corner of the coffee shop. Stepping out of the restroom, where she dabbed coffee dribble off of her work shirt, she froze when she recognized the man at the counter.

Not intending to spy, just stay out of sight, she couldn't

help but to overhear and witness the exchange. A flood of emotions, from anger and resentment, to kindness, to heartbreak to confusion overwhelmed her. Fighting through them all, she marched through the coffee shop and flung the screen door open.

Hearing the telltale screech, Dean spun from his car door. He was shocked to see Shelby, even more so when she made a beeline towards him.

"What was that?" Shelby demanded. "Why did you do that?"

Dean was bewildered, "Do…what?"

"The coffee. Buy that man a drink?" Shelby asked. "You weren't just being nice to get a date!"

Dean studied the girl, trying to comprehend the tirade.

Shelby continued, talking to herself as much as she was Dean, "Maybe…maybe I'm wrong about you. Maybe you are simply a nice guy…"

She looked directly into Dean's eyes. Her frustration boiled over. Her own eyes betrayed the realization that she had no idea why she was confronting him.

As Dean continued to search her eyes, he found a fissure of deep-seated, weary pain amidst the stunning brilliance.

Taking a deep breath, he responded, "The truth is, the guy you thought I was, I probably used to be. He's a guy I wouldn't want you…or anyone else to like. Not so sure I like him very much."

Shelby's outburst diffused. She stood staring at Dean, unsure how she'd found herself standing there.

"I'm a long way from perfect. A long way from the man I'd like to be, but I take steps every day to remind myself. Buying a veteran a coffee, shaking their hand. Appreciating people who sacrifice a whole lot more than I ever sniffed, kind of puts things in perspective," Dean admitted.

For a long moment, the two stared at each other without saying a word. Neither knew what to do or say next.

Finally, Dean blurted, "The woman last night, she was an old friend. Celebrating with friends before going home to her husband and children." As the words came out, he realized he wasn't sure why he felt compelled to share that fact.

Shelby sighed, "Tomorrow night, my schedule got messed up. I'm off at six."

"Uhm, okay..."

"I still owe you from the grocery store," Shelby snapped.

"Right," Dean nodded. "I'll pick you up at six."

"At the restaurant," Shelby said quickly. She was not going to share her home address.

"I'll see you then," Dean said, still somewhat confused about the entire conversation.

Without another word, Shelby spun and retreated into the

coffee shop. The screen door slapped shut behind her. She stood frozen, a hand on her forehead, trying to rest herself.

Having heard the exchange between Olivia and Dean, Shelby asked, "Do you know that man?"

"No, not really, just comes in each morning," Olivia admitted. "Seems nice."

"Yeah. *Seems* nice," Shelby nodded warily.

Dean sat at the desk in the beach house room that he had claimed for his office. He had everything that he needed to dive into his work, yet he struggled to focus on completing his analysis for updating the contract. He found himself thinking about the odd exchange with Shelby. Her judgment of him and the admitted accuracy of his past-self ate at him. He found himself inundated with images and conversations from the past, especially those of Allie.

Instead of breaking down a spreadsheet, the search engine on his laptop drew his attention. Putting in names from college, he began noting who still had ties to Wilmington. His mind picked off one person after another– anyone he regretted how he treated when he was there or on his way out.

After assembling a list with possible locations, he grabbed his keys and headed out. Dean wasn't sure what he was going to do or what he would say, but he felt compelled to track each one down. Deserved or otherwise, he would come to terms and address them all, confronting his past head-on.

Driving to his first stop, an antebellum country club, Dean was stymied. He had no idea what to expect. He felt miserably awkward, pulled by a string tugged from the recesses of his mind. He found himself face to face with Becca Woodburn. An elegant southern belle that, in retrospect, annoyed Dean by being too overtly southern. She smiled in surprise at her visitor.

"Oh, my sweet Lord, Dean Taylor in the living flesh," Becca sang as he walked into the country club. Stepping out from behind the desk she was sitting at, she ran up to him, with arms stretched out.

Surprised, he requited and gave her a quick hug until she pulled away to give him a once over. "What on earth are you doing here?"

"I was back in town for business, and I saw that you were running the charity program for the Azalea Festival," Dean shared. "I thought I'd come and make a donation."

Becca gushed, "That's wonderful. The charity this year is supporting foster children and their families. Something I got involved in right after college."

"Sounds like it will go to good use," Dean acknowledged.

"It will," Becca nodded. "Come on. Let's catch up over an iced tea. Though I think maybe it should be the Long Island type, goodness."

Letting her associate know she'd be back, she led Dean to the country club bar and then out to the back veranda, which overlooked the beautiful land and waterscapes of the property.

"Dean Taylor back in town," Becca shook her head. "Never thought I'd see that day."

"Me either," Dean confessed. "But it's been good to be back."

He shared his work with the negotiations and working with Cassie at Cape Fear Commercial. Dean discussed his life in California and his rise with Dana Holdings. Becca, in turn, shared her advances in Wilmington's social status with the ladies' auxiliary. Mostly, she beamed about how she'd learned to use her social connections to good work, like her current effort with the foster children.

With a few sips of iced tea left, Dean sighed and looked at Becca intently. "Listen, part of my reason for looking you up, is to say I'm sorry. I truly cared about you, and I'm ashamed of how I left things."

Becca smiled and placed a hand on his shoulder, "*Child*, we were kids. We all made our mistakes. It's all part of growing up, cutting our teeth on how relationships work, or shouldn't work for that matter."

"I appreciate that. Being back in town got me thinking about the people that left behind. Good people, I want to try to make amends with," Dean declared.

The hand on his shoulder turned into two as she drew him in for a hug, "It's good to see you. Look me up the next time you are in town."

Dean made good with his donation and settled back in the Aston Martin. With a deep breath, he plugged the next destination into his GPS.

"Marlena Davis," Dean called into the security pad at the school office.

A moment later, he heard a buzz and the latch release. Swinging the door open, he walked into the air-conditioned office. A receptionist sat behind a desk as soon as he entered the lobby.

"Do you have an appointment, sir? I don't see you on the schedule. We don't get a lot of visitors this time of year," the woman noted, eyeing Dean warily.

"No appointment necessary for this one, though we might need to rethink the security policy," a voice called from the hallway.

Dean turned, "Hello, Marlena."

"Hello, Dean," the woman in the hall called. "He's okay, Joyce. Thank you."

Turning to give Dean a solid once over, she beckoned, "Come on. We can walk."

Dean gave Joyce a quick nod and followed Marlena.

"This is a surprise," Marlena said as she led him down the school hallways.

"For me, too," Dean admitted. "I'm in town working with Cape Fear Commercial, and I saw your name in an article, Teacher of the Year, quite the accomplishment."

"My kids deserve the credit. They give me the incentive that I need each day to give them my best," Marlena declared. "You came all the way here to congratulate me?"

Dean was taken aback by the directness of the question, "Well, I... No." Swallowing, he paused, and the two stood looking at each other in the dark school hallway, strangely reminiscent of a similar moment in their history. "I, uh, have been working through some things in my own life. I... I wanted to say I'm sorry."

"For leaving? For not emailing, saying hello over social media, or sending a Christmas card? For dumping me?" Marlena recited.

"Yeah," Dean nodded, "For all of that."

Marlena giggled and placed a hand on his chest, "You always were a mushy one."

Dean frowned.

"All that sucked at the time. You hurt me. I thought, you know, you could have been the one, but the closer we got, the further you moved away," Marlena declared. "Until you finally, really moved away."

"I'm sorry. North Carolina is your home. It always will be.

I… I had to get away."

"I know. You said that on our first date. I didn't want to listen. I wanted to convince you to stay. It was wrong of me to demand that," Marlena conceded. "I suppose in that way; I'm sorry too."

Dean stared at her for a moment, absorbing her words. "You always were sweet and to the point."

"And you were sweet enough to say what I wanted to hear, but cruel enough to take it all away when the time came," Marlena scowled.

Dean could do nothing but nod. The internal torment must have been painfully evident.

"It's okay, Dean. I forgave, if not forgot that a long time ago," Marlena said. "Thank you, though, for caring enough to seek me out and tell me that. It's kind of nice, if a bit silly."

Dean didn't know where to take the conversation, but Marlena bailed him out. "I'm decorating my classroom for the start of the next school year. I'm trying to get it done before I go on vacation. I could use some help, if you're game," she suggested.

"Yeah, sure. I'd love to," Dean agreed, following her to her classroom.

Over the next hour, they decorated bulletin boards with background themes and borders. Dean climbed on desks lining the room with alphabet and number line borders. Together, they shared stories from their past and filled in gaps over the past decade. Laughing when Dean nearly fell off the desk just as he seated the ultimate staple in his efforts.

Taking a step back, they both admired their handiwork. Marlena hugged Dean as he excused himself and left to her to tidy up the finishing touches before she closed up her room for vacation.

Dean slunk his way back through the school halls, past the receptionist, and into his car. Following the navigation system's instructions to his next stop, he took a deep breath and got out of the vehicle. He was a little surprised where the map had brought him- a modern building perched right alongside the Intracoastal Waterway.

On the front window was the picture of a woman with half a dozen medals hanging from her neck. "Hmm!" Dean muttered to himself.

Pulling open the door, a scurry of people milled about. A young man in a polo shirt, with a headset attached to his ear, paused and strode over to Dean, "Can I help you, sir? Miss O'Dea doesn't meet with fans except at official events. Here take this signed photo. We appreciate your support."

Dean studied the photo, confusion across his face, "I'm not a fan… I mean, maybe I am, but that's not why I'm here."

"Sir?"

"That headset work? Let her know Dean Taylor is here."

The man frowned, "I don't think...I'll try."

Turning away, the man spoke into his headset, nodded a few times, and spun back to face Dean. "Wait right here. Miss O'Dea will be right out."

Dean waited with his hands clasped behind his back, taking in the room. Trophies and medals filled a glass case. Photos with Jenn O'Dea and a variety of celebrities adorned the walls. A flat-screen monitor played a montage of her on podiums, at events and mostly, crewing racing sailboats.

Soon, the sea of personnel parted, and Jenn O'Dea marched up towards Dean with a broad smile across her modelesque face. Her silken hair flowed behind her, and her sculpted body was smartly clothed in a summery pant-suit.

A step from Dean, she suddenly struck out with a lightning-quick swipe at his face, an open palm hitting him square on the cheek. Her smile never diminishing, perhaps even widening, she stopped.

"Now that *that's* out of the way," she grinned, "It's great to see you, Dean. What can I do for you?"

Stymied, Dean stuttered, "I...uh, I..."

"Oh, come on," Jenn cut him off and grabbed him by the hand. "Let's go back to my office. We'll catch up."

"Right," Dean nodded, working his jaw where her hand had been.

The silent crew froze in their spots as they observed the

exchange between their boss and the newcomer. Their heads swiveled as Jenn and Dean passed.

Behind Jenn's closed office door, she pointed towards a pair of chairs looking out over the Intracoastal Waterway, where a series of yachts moored along the shore.

"Dean Taylor, my word, look at you," Jenn asked. "You want a drink or something?"

Dean rubbed his cheek, "I might."

Jenn studied him for a moment, "Oh come on. You've handled worse. Remember the guy in that bar?"

"The one who tried to get handsy with you? Yeah, I remember," Dean nodded.

"He must have been twice your size, but that didn't stop you from laying him out," Jenn observed. "Always chivalrous, right up to the point it was time to break up."

"Yeah," Dean agreed, "That's kind of what led me here. I'm sorry for the way I handled things back then."

Jenn studied him for a moment, "Oh my, gosh. You're sincere. How cute!"

Dean was perturbed at the response.

Waving him off, Jenn declared, "I don't mean it like that. Since I started winning races and well…becoming purportedly famous, guys have come out of the woodwork suddenly regretting breaking up with me, magically wanting second chances. Funny what having your face on a Wheaties box or television commercial will do for your dating life."

Dean frowned, "I don't regret breaking up with you, just how I did. I mean…"

Jenn smiled, "I get it. Thank you, it's sweet. And you should be sorry."

"Kind of deserved that slap, huh?"

"And then some," Jenn nodded. "Thought about kneeing you right in the groin."

"Glad you didn't."

"What are you doing back here, anyway?" Jenn asked.

Dean shrugged, "Business with Cape Fear Commerical."

A knock on the door broke up the conversation, acknowledging the interruption, a head poked in, "I'm sorry, Miss O'Dea. The writer from Sports Illustrated is calling in for their interview."

Jenn waved him off, "I'll take it in the conference room. Buy me a minute, will you?"

The door shut, and Jenn took a good look at Dean, "I'm sorry to cut this short. It was good to connect finally."

Dean laughed, "Yes, it was. I'm glad you're doing so well."

"Life's been good to me, I can't complain. You seem to be well yourself," Jenn said. "If that Cape Fear thing turns out, let me know, I'll give you an endorsement."

Dean thanked her and followed her out to the lobby. Pausing before disappearing into the conference, she pulled him in for a warm hug.

Dean was unsure about the GPS's instructions. Having taken him way out from Wilmington and away from the coast, it led him from a rural route to a long dirt road. Coming upon a narrow drive, he guided the luxury car carefully over a few ruts in the dirt road.

A blur of brown shapes quickly met him along the drive. Giving chase, several seemingly furious dogs worked to keep him at bay. As he closed in on the house, several men were pouring over the engine bay of a raised pick up. Each stopped and eyed him as he came up the drive, their heads swiveling as he pulled closer.

A woman in overalls, her wild red hair framing an attractive face stepped out on the front porch. Readying to put the car in park, one of the men reached into the pickup and grabbed a shotgun. He took several strides toward the convertible. Seeing him, Dean cranked the wheel on the Aston and pressed the accelerator.

With a spray of gravel, the performance car raced away, putting the house, the men, and the dogs in Dean's rearview mirror. As he hit the main road, the car spun sideways into its proper lane. Wiping his brow, Dean muttered, "We'll just take that one off of the list."

Back on the main roads and far away from guns pointed in

his direction, Dean glanced at his list.

After his last rural experience, he was starting to rethink his list. Unsure he wanted to tempt another address in the country. He relented as the next was near. Following the GPS, he found a paved road running along a rambling white fence that eventually led to a large farm. Best several barns and a large garage housing several machines, he pulled next to a well-manicured house.

A tractor chugged from a nearby field, pulling alongside the driveway. A chiseled man, roughly Dean's age, hopped off of the machine, tossing his gloves on the seat. Making a beeline for Dean, the man called, "Can I help you?"

"Yeah, I'm, uh…I'm looking for…," Dean started.

"Holy hog nuts! Dean Taylor?" cheerily chirped the man as he picked up the pace.

As the man neared, Dean recognized him. "Johnny Bezold?"

"Well, you are at Bezold Farms, the second-largest hog farmer in North Carolina. Which, I hate to brag, is a pretty big deal!" Johnny beamed.

"Wow, it's terrific to see you," Dean proclaimed. "All this is yours, huh?"

Johnny grinned, "As we like to say, that pig smell smells like a million bucks."

"Impressive. I followed that fence line for miles," Dean said.

"With all the trucks hauling pigs, I finally got that road paved a few years back. So, what brings you out here?" Johnny asked.

Dean shrugged, "Looking up old friends while working on a project for Cape Fear Commercial. I was also looking for Margaret Kennedy. Does she live out this way somewhere?"

"Uh, Mags? Yeah, I hope so. I married her," Johnny grinned.

Dean's eyes widened, "You and Margaret... You always had a crush on her. Good for you."

"She's kind of the brains behind this operation. I supply the brawn. It was her idea to take her daddy's small farm, put a little investment into it, make the right connections to the big food houses and bam...Bezold Farms is on the map," Johnny said. "Let me get Mags. We'll sit and have a lemonade or somethin'. But first I gotta...Sooey! Sooey! Here piggy, piggy pig, pig!"

The front door to the immaculate farmhouse flew open, and an attractive woman in jeans and a button-down plaid shirt rolled up to the elbows burst through. "Did Sue get out again?"

"Yeah, baby. Probably off to Johnson's farm to find her boyfriend again," Johnny surmised. "Hey, look who's here."

"What the hog dropping? Dean Taylor? What in the world are you doing here?" Margaret exclaimed.

"Hey, why don't you get him some lemonade and catch up? I'll see if I can't wrangle Miss Sue back home," Johnny suggested.

"Dean, great to see you if ain't back by the time you need to push off. But let's catch up. We'll treat you to a real Carolina feast."

"Sounds good, Johnny. Good luck with Sue," Dean said.

"Well, come on in. You'll find a side effect of living on a pig farm is the black flies like living out here too," Margaret said.

Dean followed her inside the impressive house. The interior was surprisingly chic. Stone floors flowed while framed by exposed wood timbers throughout the entirety of the house. Leading him to a large gourmet kitchen, she grabbed a pitcher and filled it with ice and lemonade.

"You and Johnny," Dean grinned. "You did good. He always had a heart of gold."

"You two were close in school, weren't you?" Margaret said.

Dean nodded, "We were."

"I don't recall him mentioning you since graduation," Margaret observed.

"Yeah," Dean admitted with a sullen drop of his head. "Moving to California, I got sucked into my job at a big firm. That's what brought me out here. Just not a lot of time for socializing, I guess."

"Oh, we understand it. Making this farm what it is was quite the undertaking. Lost track of a few folks along the way ourselves, I suppose. Especially living way out here," Margaret shared. "How'd you find us?"

"Had an off day. Figured I'd use it to look up who I could,"

Dean said.

"And you found us?"

"Yeah, I read you owned a farm, I had no idea the scale. You must be proud of what you and Johnny built," Dean said.

"The working together to build something was on purpose. The scale we just kind of lucked into it. Made the right connections is all," Margaret shared.

Dean shifted in his seat, "Part of why I'm making the rounds is to, well, apologize."

Margaret frowned, "Apologize for what?"

"I guess I should apologize to the both of you. I knew Johnny had a crush on you, but I still asked you out anyway. That was kind of crummy. And, well, I never told you I broke up with you because, uh, I didn't feel I fit with your family," Dean screwed his face into a knot as he admitted his story to her.

Margaret stared at him for a moment before bursting into laughter. "I was horrified you would meet my family. The rash they would give me about dating a soft city boy like you? That would've been rough," Margaret shared.

Dean's face fell as he processed the reverse scenario. Finally, he erupted into laughter as well.

"Johnny was bad enough, but that boy works his tail off. Initially, I think it was just to impress me, but he took to it. Daddy fell in love with him before I did, I think," Margaret recalled.

"He's a good guy. Always has been," Dean said.

"He is," Margaret said. "He doesn't know it yet, but there is a little Johnny or Mags in here," she shared, patting her belly.

"Congratulations," Dean beamed. "Wow, a little Johnny running around. You're going to have your hands full."

"You're telling me," Margaret nodded. "Listen, I'm sure Johnny would love to visit with you. But knowing him and Sue and the Johnsons, that is not going to be a short trip. Come by again sometime? Like he said, we'd treat you to one heck of a feast."

"Sounds good. Thank you for the lemonade. I'm really happy for you two…three," Dean said, getting up. Leaning in, he gave Margaret a quick hug. "Tell Johnny we'll catch up."

"I will. Don't be a stranger, okay?"

"I won't," Dean promised and let himself out.

Driving away, he smiled. He couldn't be happier for his college friend. Johnny was always the shy, somewhat awkward wingman. To see that he settled down and was starting a family with the girl he had a crush on made Dean very happy.

He gave a wave to Margaret, who peered out of the front door at him, and he backed out of the driveway.

The next two names brought him back into Wilmington. Following the GPS, he was surprised when it led him to a big office building downtown. Taking a second glance at the address, he confirmed that he was in the right place.

Brianna Caits was adorable as a button, but her lack of

ambition drove Dean crazy. As he ascended the steps of the office building, he wondered if Brianna was a receptionist or executive assistant. She could undoubtedly charm her way to holding a job.

Entering the building, a cheery girl behind a glass desk greeted him. Behind her, a wall of monitors linked together, showing video loops of clouds billowing by her. Upbeat, modern instrumental music piped through expensive speakers giving the office a trendy, high-end vibe.

"Can I help you, sir?" the girl asked. Looking like one of the models in the company ads that lined either wall alongside the foyer, she smiled patiently for Dean's response.

"Yes, I'm not sure I have the right address, but I am looking for Brianna Caits," Dean replied.

The girl broke into a broad smile, "It's the right address, Carolina Girl Cosmetics is Brianna's company."

"I see," Dean tried to hide his surprise and confusion. "Would it be possible to see her if she has a moment. I'm an old friend from college."

"I'm sorry. Ms. Caits is in Milan. She'll be back in about two weeks," the girls said, looking at her digital schedule. "No, then she's in Paris for a week and then the show in New York. Maybe I can get your information and have her reach back out to you?"

Stymied, Dean didn't know how to respond. "Yeah, sure." Absently, he handed his card from Dana Holdings. "Thank you."

"I'll be sure to get this to her," the girl said half-heartedly. "Bye, now."

Nodding, Dean made his way out of the building.

He played with the scenarios of the day. None of them matched his expectations, except for maybe Jenn's reaction. He sighed as he sat in his car. The final name- circled in heavy ink on the list, gave him pause. He knew in his heart that this name was the one that compelled him to undertake the exercise in the first place.

He chewed on his lip as he drove towards his next Wilmington stop. Ten years of being plagued with random images of her popped into his head. Each time, his heart would sink The look on her face when he left her. The broken promises. The building up of his gallantry only to fail so catastrophically, he embodied everything that he professed not to be to her.

Pulling outside of her office building, he started to contemplate the merits of his day. Was he only acting even more selfish by injecting him into people's lives? He knew they had moved on. He closed his eyes, deciding what he should do.

Startled, he was brought out of his thoughts by a light knocking at his car window. Turning his head, he saw Allie looking back at him. Rolling down the window, he gave her a sheepish smile.

"Are you going to sit out here all day? It's hot out," Allie said.

"It's not so bad, air conditioning runs cold. These seats are super comfortable," Dean said.

"I was about to get a cold beverage. How about you join me," Allie asked.

Nonchalantly, Dean nodded his head, "Yeah, sure. That'd be fine too."

Rolling up his window, he shut the Aston Martin off and got out of the vehicle.

"Wow, nothing for ten years and now three times in a week," Allie said, "What are the odds?"

Dean shuffled as he glanced at his feet, "This time was intentional."

"I figured as much," Allie said. Congenially, she nodded her head toward the sidewalk, "Come on. Let's get that cold drink."

Dean followed from his car and down the walkway.

"So, what's up?" Allie asked.

"I, uh, I have to admit… coming back here… It hasn't been easy for me," Dean said. "The moment I crossed I-95, you popped in my head…not in a weird way…but, in an I feel like a jerk kind of way."

"I see, I kind of gathered that the other night when I had my arms full of dry cleaning," Allie nodded.

They stopped and faced each other.

"Look, I feel terrible about how I treated you. Every time I think of mistakes in my life, you're the image that comes to mind...," Dean began.

"Thanks," Allie grimaced.

Dean waved her off, "No, not like that. How I acted. I was so scared that someone, someone like you would keep me from leaving. I fought it with everything I had. I am sorry you were in the crosshairs of that. I cared way more for you than demonstrated in how I treated you. You deserved more. Way more than that, and I am sorry."

Dean's last words fluttered out in a hoarse rasp.

"Wow, you have been holding on to that for a long time," Allie said. "Dean, I've moved on, probably just shy of ten years ago."

"I know I have no doubts. I just wanted, needed to share how sorry I am," Dean said contritely.

Allie laughed, raising an eyebrow. "Wow, you really think highly of yourself. Did you think you were weighing on my mind all the years, all sad and brooding? I wasn't sad, Dean. I was disappointed in you. You let me down. You let *yourself* down."

She studied him for a moment, "People do stupid things when they are scared or need to break away. It sounds like you did all of those things. Don't get me wrong. I'm not excusing you for what you did or how you acted. But Dean, I forgave you a long time ago."

"I guess I haven't forgiven myself," Dean said.

"My pastor says the first step towards real redemption is confessing your sins publicly," Allie said. Her eyes suddenly brightened, "Hey, why don't you join us for church on Sunday?"

Dean shuffled his feet, "I don't know, I don't want to interfere…"

"You won't be interfering. In fact, why don't you join my family for dinner tonight? You remember Thomas Holmes?" Allie asked.

Dean frowned, searching his memory banks, "Thomas…"

"He said in high school you saved him from a kid who was bullying him," Allie said.

"Tommy Holmes… Yes! I think I gave the kid… Bobby, a black eye. Wasn't much of a guy to get into fights, but yeah, I remember little Tommy. Couldn't let him be pushed around like that," Dean said.

"Well, he's my husband now. In fact, that who I was meeting for an afternoon break. Come on. I'm sure he'd love to see you," Allie pressed.

"Why would he love to see *me*?" Dean asked.

"Why wouldn't he?" Allie grinned. "He got the girl."

Dean tilted his head to the side, relenting, "Alright."

Holding the door open for Allie, they walked into the coffee shop. A man sitting at a table perked up and came over. Kissing his wife on the cheek, he recognized that someone was in tow with her.

Giving him a quick glance, he said, "Dean Taylor." Holding out his hand to Dean, they shook.

"It's good to see you. I see you found Allie," Thomas said. "She told me she ran into you, literally. Come on. Let me buy you a drink or something."

"Thomas, you're looking good. I'd love to visit, but only if I can get you something," Dean insisted.

"Sure," Thomas said.

"I was telling Dean he should come over for dinner, meet the kids," Allie informed her husband.

"Yeah, that would be great. I've got some steaks in the fridge, just as easy to add one more on the grill," Thomas said.

Dean's head spun with the reaction from the pair. It was certainly not what he expected. "Yeah," he nodded absently, "That would be great."

Ordering iced teas, Dean was suddenly overwhelmed, "Hey, I don't want to horn in your afternoon visit. I, uh, I'll look forward to dinner."

"You bet, absolutely. Here's my card. Give me a text, and I'll send you the address," Thomas said.

Dean accepted the card, excused himself, and left the coffee shop as quickly, and smoothly as he could.

"So, you spent the morning on what? An apology tour?" Cassie snorted.

Dean was beside himself, "I had to do something."

"You didn't have to do *that*," Cassie chuckled. "Was it because we had our little moment over lunch?"

Dean shook his head, "No. I mean, somewhat. It's more than that. I need to take responsibility for my actions."

"From when you were little more than a child?" Cassie asked.

"It's more than that. How I treated Allie Caylor…Holmes, now… It has haunted me for years."

"Let me get this straight. You entered all of these women's, and now their families, lives so you could feel better about yourself? Dean, you're still sweet, but that seems like just a different type of selfish than you were ten years ago," Cassie scoffed.

Dean frowned, "I hadn't thought of it that way."

"Look, anyone who knew you well enough, knew you were a nice guy. All guys, at certain points of their lives and unfortunately, in their relationships, they go haywire and act like a jerk. You're part of a massive club. What made you feel so special?" Cassie pressed.

"I guess I had higher expectations for myself," Dean admitted.

"Okay, I can respect that," Cassie nodded. "So, what happened with Allie? Why is she, of all your conquests, the one that haunts your dreams at night?"

Dean looked thoughtful for a moment, "She came to me at

a tender time. She and Mark had broken up. I professed to be everything that he wasn't. I put that badge on and when push came to shove..."

"You acted just like him."

"Worse."

"And how did your apology visit with Allie go?"

"Uhm, she invited me to dinner, and I bought her husband an iced tea...," Dean said.

Cassie covered her mouth as she stifled a laugh, "Let me guess. You expected some virulent reaction. Instead, you were invited to dinner?"

"Yeah, that's about right," Dean nodded sullenly.

"So, get over it. Everyone else has," Cassie said.

"It's that easy?"

"Why not? Are you looking to come back and sweep any of your lists of girls you treated poorly off their feet and marry them?" Cassie asked.

"No. But I want them to know I'm sorry for treating them the way I did," Dean said.

"For you or them?"

"I thought for them."

"But it's not, Dean. Trust me when I tell you, I am *well* over the past. You need to get there too. I'm sorry you did dumb things. Truth is, we all did," Cassie said. "You need to feel better about yourself. Man up. Own your mistakes, move on, and never do them again. That's all you can do. That's life."

"Thank you for listening to me and putting up with me this week," Dean said.

"Dean, it's been really good to spend time with you. I miss you as a friend," Cassie said. With a stern twinge in her voice, she added, "I hope you mean what you say when it comes to this business and the people throughout North Carolina that Cape Fear Commercial represents."

"I do," Dean nodded.

"Then we're good. Enjoy your dinner with your ex-girlfriend and her husband," Cassie winked, leaving him to collect his thoughts on the back patio of the office building.

Dean watched Cassie get into her SUV and drive away.

With a hand on the porch rail, he paused, deciphering his next step. Out of the corner of his eye, he noticed a figure approaching from the slightly opened rear door of the office. Bart Stevens strode out.

"Forgive me, Dean," Stevens announced himself. "I couldn't help but overhear. It sounds as though you have had an interesting return home."

Embarrassed, Dean admitted, "Yes, sir. I have."

"Don't mean to intrude on your personal affairs, but in the context of your character and how it may relate to our business, I find it speaks volumes," Stevens said.

Dean looked confused, "I am not sure I follow, sir."

"In business, like in life, we all make mistakes and continue to. It's our nature as earthbound creatures. It is how we hold ourselves in the aftermath of those mistakes that defines our character. Flawed or not, I find your somewhat ill-advised journey an…interesting mark on your character," Stevens shared.

"'Interesting' can go a number of different ways," Dean said.

Stevens gave a hearty laugh, "That it can. As in, I find it interesting that you are still here. Going through the motions to satisfy a silly old man's requirements to complete a business transaction."

"It is a bit out of the ordinary," Dean admitted.

"I don't necessarily need the best financial deal, don't get me wrong. I'm not changing the terms at this point. I *do* need to make a deal with a company that has Cape Fear's people at heart," Mr. Stevens said. "You're reconciling your past, right or wrong, shows that you carry people's hearts with you. You carried a piece of them with you. You never let them go. That is what separates gentlemen of character from those lacking. With over three-thousand miles of landscape, you could have buried those memories anywhere along the way."

Dean looked contrite. "Maybe I did, sir. I just happened to dig them up on my way back here."

"From my observation, if that were the case, it wouldn't weigh on you quite so much," Stevens pressed.

Surprising himself, with the words as they tumbled out, Dean said, "Then what would you suggest I do?"

Mr. Stevens smiled. "Let's talk and walk."

The conversation with his prospective client was certainly not anything that Dean had planned. The idea of it, in Dean's mind, was absurd on many levels. On the other hand, he found Mr. Stevens a reasonable man and their conversations pleasant. He also understood that from Mr. Stevens' perspective, it was an excellent opportunity to vet his company's suitor.

Without sharing any great detail, Dean shared what plagued with him, addressing his past on the highest level. He wasn't even sure how Shelby had come up in conversation about weekend plans. Mr. Stevens picked up a change in Dean's tenor when the conversation moved in that direction.

Pressing in, Mr. Stevens challenged Dean to look at his interactions with her this past week versus the ten years ago version of himself.

"We learn from our mistakes, Dean. You carried yours with you. You hit them head-on this week and continue to. Listening to your stories, which I have very much enjoyed and appreciated you sharing, I hear your younger selfish-self battling your more mature selfless- self. Out of that, you get to enjoy a date this weekend without any expectations," Mr. Stevens suggested.

"It's just dinner, not really a date," Dean protested.

"That fits my point exactly. What would your younger self have called it?"

"A date."

Mr. Stevens smiled.

"It's been a pleasure speaking with you, sir," Dean said as they arrived back at the office parking lot.

"Likewise," Mr. Stevens extended his hand. "Any time, regardless of how our business transaction turns out."

With a wave, Dean started his rented sports car and pulled away from the office and towards the beach.

Chapter Fourteen -
A Date with an Ex...and Her Husband

Dean wasn't sure why he was nervous about visiting Allie's family for dinner, but he was. The evening was brilliant as he drove across the Wrightsville Beach bridge and the short drive to Masonboro, an estuary streaked residential area between the coast and downtown Wilmington.

The GPS guided him to the address on his screen. There was a mini-van parked in the driveway. The sounds of children playing and giggling rang from the backyard. Grabbing the bag of treats he had picked up from the Cotton Exchange shops and a bottle of wine, he strode up to Allie and Thomas' front door.

Ringing the doorbell, Dean waited awkwardly, waving toward a neighbor walking their dog, who took a keen interest in the Holmes' visitor. His wait wasn't long as Thomas swung the door open, two children at his heels.

"You found us," Thomas beamed. "This is Clarice and Ben. Kids, this is Dean, a friend from your mom's and my school days."

"Hi, guys!" Dean smiled at the kids, each peeking out from either of their father's legs. They ran off in a fit of giggles.

"They'll be in your lap by the end of the evening," Thomas informed him.

Dean was unclear whether that was an assurance or a warning. Following his host through the house and into an open kitchen, he found Allie chopping vegetables.

Allie looked up and smiled, "I'm so glad you made it. I could tell from the squeals that you met Clarice and Ben."

"I did," Dean nodded. "They're beautiful."

"Thank goodness they take after their mother," Thomas grinned, winking at his wife.

"I, uh, brought some treats for after dinner…and some wine. I- I don't know if you…," Dean stammered.

"Honey, will you open that up for Dean and pour a few glasses," Allie suggested as her husband snapped into action.

Dean sat on a stool opposite the kitchen area and took in the scene. Aside from the sundry of toys scattered in the living room, the quaint. Nearly every wall was adorned by a combination of family photos and bible verses.

"Allie tells me you are working on a deal with Cape Fear Commercial," Thomas saod as he worked the cork out of the bottle.

"That's what brought me out here, yes," Dean acknowledged.

"Good company."

"What... What do you do, Thomas?" Dean asked.

"Insurance," Thomas answered. "Nothing glamorous like corporate acquisitions, but it provides a roof over our heads, and I get to be at all of the kids' events. How about you? Any kiddos of your own?"

Allie snorted from behind her cutting board.

Dean shot her a quick look before responding, "No, just living the California bachelor life, I guess."

"Must be nice out there, right?" Thomas asked, placing a glass in front of his wife and handing one to Dean.

"Yeah," Dean shrugged. "I like it. I work a lot, get a little surfing in, travel."

Grabbing a tray of steaks, he nodded Dean toward the screen door in the back of the house. Sliding the door open, Dean followed Thomas onto the back patio.

"Sounds like you've got a real nice life out there. Any future Mrs. Taylors on the horizon?"

"Not so far. Not sure how conducive my work life is for that right now, anyway. Maybe things will change when I make partner," Dean confessed. "I am told relationships work better when you have time to spend with one another."

Thomas nodded, pointing a meat fork towards Dean, "See,

that's why I went with insurance. Get to work in the community, set my own hours. I'm hoping by the time Ben is in Little League. I'll be doing well enough to sponsor his team."

"Sure. That's a real good goal," Dean replied, noting internally how starkly different their lives and their ambitions were. He watched the innocuous man cheerfully work the steaks on the grill and steal a glance through the screen door at Allie, who looked strangely ravishing while chopping vegetables with children hanging on either hip. His mind played with the pairing.

She looked so content with the life that she had. Thomas was a kind man, and while not exceptionally dynamic on the surface, the way he treated her, the way he so apparently loved her and their children, he was precisely the sort of man deserving of a woman like her.

Dean's thoughts consumed him thoroughly. He was startled when Thomas stood in front of him, a heaping tray of steaks wafting in the air. Snapping out of it, Dean lunged for the door, sliding it open.

Seated around the dining table, the family reached their arms out, hands open on either side of them. Nestled between Allie and Clarice, Dean grasped their hands and bowed his head as Thomas said grace. Listening to him pray so gratefully for his family, for all of their needs being met and graced with their friend's visit, Dean recognized the masculinity and power within Thomas was far greater than what his outward appearance conveyed. Dean suddenly felt like half the man that this simple insurance agent was.

Throughout the meal, they caught up on life and experience since college. Most of Dean's conversation centered around his work and work-related travels while the Holmes' tale revolved around their shared experiences as a family. Dean found himself envying their past decade of stories over his own.

When the evening came to a close, and the family to a head begged him to join them for church on Sunday, Dean excused himself as the littlest Holmes was yawning profusely- as Thomas had predicted- in his lap.

"Daddy," Ben yawned sleepily, "Will you tuck me in?"

"Sure, sport!" Thomas popped out of the chair and held out his arms to accept his son.

"Goodnight, Mr. Dean," Ben said.

"Goodnight, buddy," Dean smiled.

"Clarice, you want to run up and pick out a book? I'll see Mr. Dean out," Allie suggested to her daughter.

"Okay, Mommy. Bye, Mr. Dean. See you at church Sunday!" Clarice waved as she ran for the stairs.

"See you then, Clarice. Goodnight!" Dean called.

Leading him to the door, Allie grinned, "You're good with kids."

"They're sweet," Dean admitted. "Thank you for inviting me over. I honestly wasn't sure how it would be, but I had a genuinely nice evening. You have a wonderful family."

Allie nodded, "I have a pretty charmed life."

As he got to the edge of his car, Dean turned, his eyes frowning, "Why... Why are you two so nice to me?"

Allie was taken aback for a moment, digesting the query. Frowning herself, she responded, "Why wouldn't we be?"

"Because I freaked out and treated you terribly. I acted the exact opposite of what I professed to be to you," Dean said flatly.

"You did," Allie admitted. "Because of who I trusted you to be, who I knew you to be, you were the worst for me. You were."

"Then, why?" Dean demanded.

"Because of that amazing man in there. Those precious children who fill me up every day. Because God points me on a path of grace and redemption," Allie replied.

"And Thomas?"

Allie smiled knowingly, "He knows our past... all of it. He may seem like a simple man, but behind that aw-shucks insurance agent exterior is the heart of a strong, righteous Christian man, a husband, a father. It was *his* idea to invite you to dinner."

"Why?"

Allie shrugged, "Show you a better life? No exciting travel, no sports cars that cost more than our house but a fulfilling, God-kissed life with no real wants other than what is under that roof. And to invite you to church."

"He's a good man," Dean said. "He's a very fortunate man."

"I know," Allie grinned. "You're a good man, too. I just don't think you have found that out for yourself yet."

Dean looked absently toward the house, her words resonating.

"Now get out of here, I've got a princess book to read," Allie said, her arms wide, stepping in to hug Dean.

Chapter Fifteen - Surf's Up

Dean watched the waves roll in. The surf report had been accurate. The offshore tropical depression had brought the most robust wave action since he'd arrived.

Red flags flapped overhead as he carried his surfboard past the lifeguard stand. The flag color indicated high surf and strong currents. Several families played along the edge of the water, with a few daring the shore break with bodyboards.

Halfway between Crystal Pier and his rental house, Dean found a group of surfers who found the ideal spot to line up where the waves were breaking powerful and clean. Carrying his board into the froth, he powered through the shore pound and pushed out to the swells.

Straddling his board, he bobbed along the edge of the line-up, watching the riders ahead of him tackle the strong waves. A few had smooth rides, carving their wave through until the ocean tried to ruthlessly dump them into the sand below at the expanded shore break. A few had entirely different experiences, being tossed in the air and flung into the surf or lifted and slammed headfirst into the wash.

Dean found his set and cast off. With a few vigorous strokes, he leaped on top of his board, riding it low with his knees bent to maximize his grip and lower trunk balance. At first, the wave fought him, trying to cast him off like a rodeo bull before he found the groove of smooth power in the heart of the wave. Not worrying about being artistic with his ride, he enjoyed the speed and the ability to conquer such ferocity.

As he reached the point where the waves just threatened to break, Dean hopped off while he was still able to land in the mass of the swell instead of the hollow froth and less forgiving hard sand. With a grin on his face, he pulled his board alongside and readied himself to fight the current for another ride.

Dean repeated the process, with variable results, several times. Given the extra effort required to fight the stronger waves, he enjoyed a moment beyond the swells to rest atop his board. Catching his breath, he admired the Carolina coastline. It was accessible yet peaceful. You could easily mix in with a crowd, especially near the piers if you wanted to, or find a lonely spot to enjoy nearly unfettered. The warm water and smooth-running beaches free from jagged outcroppings made for a pure experience to enjoy the waves and gentle shoreline.

Pinpointing his location versus the shore, he found the natural momentum of the current had driven he and much of the surf crowd a hundred yards horizontal to the beach where they had entered. A group of people at the shoreline caught his attention. Shielding their eyes, they scanned the waterline.

Dean's first instinct was to look for a fin writhing along the surface. A patch of dark water void of white froth caught his attention, and he quickly understood. They were approaching a rip current. Occasionally, frantic hands would breach the water only for the ocean to pull them back down, each interval further apart and less fervent.

Dean quickly unleashed the tether around his ankle and dove off his board. Swimming directly toward the current, he used several strokes under the water to rush in the direction of the flailing hands. Taking an angle from where he last spied the swimmer to deeper water, Dean made quick gains. Rising to the surface, he could feel the tug offshore. Dean knew he was in the current. Swiveling desperately, he searched for the swimmer.

Diving under the water, he opened his eyes, ignoring the sting of salt as he searched of skin or the flash of a bathing suit. From his vantage while on the surfboard, he noticed a slight bend in the current deeper out to sea and angling toward the pier. Knowing that was where the current would eventually deposit the swimmer, he made a beeline, using the current to his advantage.

Bobbing at the end of the curve, he spied the hunched back of the swimmer floating face down.

Wasting no time, Dean caught up in a few strong strokes and, with one arm, hooked the swimmer's waist pulling him free from the rip current and toward the shoreline. By the time he was able to rest with his knees in the sandy shore break, hands pulled the boy away and carried him up to the beach. Others stayed to ensure Dean was okay.

Waving them off, Dean collected himself and made the rest of his way to the beach where a crowd had assembled to deliver medical care to the child. In moments, to the relief of Dean and everyone else, the boy started coughing with a volume of saltwater expelling from his lungs.

The beach erupted in cheers as the boy sat up, enveloped in hugs from his parents. Satisfied the boy was okay and in good hands. Dean left the family their space to reconcile the near tragedy and rejoice in being together safely, loving on one another. With a half-hearted scan of the ocean, he searched for his surfboard, knowing he might never see it again.

His day on the water was done. Dean slipped away from the crowd in the direction of his beach house. As he separated from the throng of caretakers and onlookers, leaving silent footsteps in the sand, he failed to sense a pair of eyes high up on Crystal Pier quietly observing the scene and watching him walk away.

Chapter Sixteen -
A Reluctant Date

As nervous as he was visiting Allie and Thomas the previous evening, Dean was surprisingly less so as he parked in front of the restaurant at the Crystal Pier. Whether it was the day's excitement putting life into perspective or the fact that he just plain did not know what to expect from the evening and the curt, defiant single mother, Dean found his heart beating in irregular rhythms as he wiped his palms against his pants.

The double doors flung open as he ascended the restaurant steps. In the midst of foyer stood Shelby, frozen as she stared out at Dean coming to greet her. Despite the now-familiar perturbed scowl and an arm full of work clothes, she was stunning. She wore a flowing sundress and her hair was down instead of the ponytail that Dean was used to seeing.

The fact that her coworkers were on either side of the door

did not appear to sit well with Shelby, and she seemed more abrupt than usual. "Well, you can't say I don't pay my debts," she said to Dean as she strode forward. Eyeing the ladies who flashed suspect grins as she passed, "Thank you, girls, and no, this isn't a date."

Dean held his arm out for Shelby as she whisked by. "Do you mind if I dump this stuff in my car? Or I could just follow you, if you prefer," Shelby suggested.

"No, it's fine," Dean said.

Marching to her car, Shelby opened the passenger door, tossed her clothes inside and grabbed a pair of sunglasses from the dash.

Dean stood by in the drive, waiting patiently. A glance at her license plate suddenly struck him. The gold star to the left of her alphanumeric sounded loud and clear. Shelby was a single mother because she lost her husband in military conflict.

Dean sighed and dropped his head slightly. He tried to reconcile what little he'd observed and formulated about this woman. She wasn't angry at men *because* of a man. She was angry at the world because of a *good* man.

His mind reeled, not knowing how to address her loss, deciding it would be up to her to bring it up, if she chose to. Snapping his head out of his thoughts as he caught Shelby giving him a quizzical glance, he led her to the convertible.

Shelby stared at the expensive car for a moment as if determining whether she wanted to get into it. She seemed to look at it with the same disdain as if it were a messy rust bucket. Dean held the door open for her and waited without a word. Without offering him a glance or uttering a sound, she slid into the car.

Dean suddenly felt very strange about his decision to rent such an ostentatious car. As he settled into his seat, he asked, almost as if he were embarrassed, "Top-down or top-up?"

Shelby seemed to brighten, just briefly. "You know, down sounds nice."

Complying, Dean started the car and lowered the top. "Where to?"

"I don't know. Outside of the restaurant I work at, I have not eaten out since I moved here, unless you count Chick-fil-A?" Shelby admitted. "Do you have a plan?"

Dean wrinkled his nose, "Well, not a plan, but an idea."

Putting the Aston Martin in gear, he pulled out of the restaurant parking lot and pointed that car towards the bridge leading across the Intracoastal Waterway.

"So, you used to live here?" Shelby asked.

Dean nodded, "Grew up south of here, came up to Wilmington for college."

"Why did you leave?"

"Question for me back then, was why wouldn't I," Dean replied.

"Ah, the small-town boy needed to escape," Shelby suggested. "Take on the big, wild world."

"Something like that," Dean admitted. "And you?"

"Grew up in Mount Olive, didn't stray too far to college. Lived just outside of Fayetteville...until about a year ago, when we moved here," Shelby said. She stared steadily out of her window as she talked with the wind gently streaming her hair backward.

Taking care not to press, Dean focused on driving as he swung the car away from the beaches and toward downtown. Much of the ride was filled the whoosh of the wind and the pleasant growl of the engine. Closing in on city center, Dean noticed the roads were busy for the time of night.

"Waterfront street fair. If you're trying to get to the restaurants on the river, you'll have to park, and we'll hoof it," Shelby said.

Dean shot her a questioning look.

"It's fine," she replied, returning her gaze straight forward through the windshield.

Finding a spot along the water's edge of the city center, he pulled in. Hopping out of his seat, he jogged around the car, where Shelby was already getting out. She shot him a look as though his attempt at chivalry was an annoyance but then acquiesced to allow him to hold the door and shut it for her.

"It's a nice night for a walk, anyways," he shrugged.

Shelby looked around as though she hadn't noticed but nodded, "It is."

Facing the Cape Fear River, he knew they only had two

options– north or south. "I guess we go this way," Dean said.

Side by side, they walked toward the boardwalk running along the water and the sounds of music played by a live band. The smells of street food began to hang in the heavy evening air.

Seeing a family sitting along the bank, skimming rocks across the river, Shelby admitted, "I saw you with that boy today. That was brave of you."

"I'm glad I was in the right place at the right time," Dean shrugged.

"Why didn't you stay to talk to the family?" Shelby wondered.

Dean's eyes also lit on the family as they walked by, "Their attention was where it should have been. That moment had nothing to do with me."

"Hmm," Shelby nodded thoughtfully.

Walking through the crowd and past the street fair, they found themselves between two restaurants, each perched right on the river's edge. "What do you think? Left or right?"

Shelby looked at the two restaurants and shrugged.

"Left," Dean said confidently and led her into the building.

A hostess met them instantly, "It's a great evening. Would you like inside window or dockside view?"

"Let's go dockside," Shelby tugged Dean towards the outside tables.

The hostess followed and led them to a table right on the

river's edge. Dean peered over the edge intently, leaning as far over the rail as he could.

"What are you looking for?" Shelby asked.

"Alligators!" Dean replied a little hop conveying a boyishness to him.

Shelby leaned in with him and studied the water, offering a soft laugh. After a minute, she turned and whispered, "I don't see any."

"Nope," Dean said, disappointment ringing his voice. "I don't either."

Relieving themselves of wildlife watching, they resigned to focus on dinner, Dean slid out a seat for Shelby who begrudgingly accepted.

Looking over the menu, Shelby looked concerned. Dean noticed.

"Why did you pick this place versus the one on the right? Just curious," Shelby asked.

"I saw through the windows that left looked a little more formal," Dean replied. "I figured with you waiting on people all that time. I thought it might be nice to have the script flipped for once."

"I don't, uh, I don't normally pay this much for food. It's kind of a single mom thing," Shelby sputtered.

Dean smiled, "It's okay. I agreed to dinner. I didn't agree you would pay for it."

Shelby's dissatisfaction washed across her face. She studied Dean with an icy glare.

"It's not like *that*, either," Dean promised.

"Fine, but I think I'll trade the wine menu for beer," Shelby tossed the book on the table defiantly.

Dean grinned as the waitress came by, "Two beers, please."

"So, what's it like being back after being gone so long?"

"It's been a reflective experience," Dean admitted after a moment to weigh his response.

"That sounds intriguing," Shelby pressed.

Shrugging, Dean replied, "Memories both good and bad. Reconciling the past, a bit."

"Did you miss it here, being gone?" Shelby asked.

"I really didn't think I did. Focused on my career and moving ahead, I didn't take much time to look back."

"No family or friends tugging you home?"

"Most of my family scattered during that time for one reason or another," Dean shrugged. He was contrite as he added, "As for friends, well, being back, I realize I may have undervalued those connections."

"Life takes over, trust me," Shelby said defending him. "Try adding two kids to the plate, and you hardly have time for a bubble bath, never mind socializing."

"Seems like you're doing great," Dean offered.

Shelby broke into a warm smile, "They're precious."

"You should do that more often," Dean suggested.

Shelby frowned, "Do what?"

"Smile."

Looking down sheepishly, she answered, "Yeah, I guess I don't do that as much since...the kids' father...my husband...died overseas."

"I'm sorry," Dean bowed his head slightly.

Shelby suddenly looked suspicious, "Is that why you did that at the coffee shop?"

Dean looked confused, "Did what?"

"Stopped and talked to that veteran, because that might impress the widow?" Shelby asked accusingly.

"You were watching me?" Dean frowned. "I didn't know until tonight. I saw your Gold Star license plate leaving the restaurant."

Shelby's face flushed, and she sheepishly admitted, "I was in the corner. I heard your voice, and I guess I was sort of creeping in the shadows. I'm sorry, I shouldn't have..."

"It's okay," Dean cut her off. "I can only imagine what you've been through, and well, my side of the species can be a bit insensitive."

"David was a good man. He loved his family. He loved his job, his country," Shelby shared. "He knew the risk, but I never expected him to not come home to us."

"That must have been tough," Dean said softly.

"It was… it is," Shelby nodded. Shaking herself, she looked up and grimaced, "I'm sorry. Not much of dinner date talk, is it?"

"I thought it wasn't a date," Dean smiled, raising an eyebrow.

Shelby cast a stern look, "You know what I meant."

"I know. I'm just happy to visit with you. No pretenses," Dean said.

Shelby looked as directly at him as she had the entire week, "It is nice."

"How'd you end up down here?" Dean asked.

"After the funeral, I didn't want to…I couldn't stay where everything reminded me every minute of what I lost. I took the kids on a beach getaway, and kind of never went home. My family and friends packed our stuff up. And the rest is sort of history. I didn't really plan it. Things just sort of worked out that way," Shelby shrugged.

Dean nodded, "Life can work out that way. I'm sorry for the reason that led to yours."

"It's okay. The kids and I, we're content, I would say. Apart from a pretty big hole in our lives. Most days now, we're good. Occasionally, something happens to twist the knife a bit. Never forgotten, but each day is less about being sad and more about remembering how wonderful our time with him was," Shelby admitted. "How about you? How did you end up in California?"

Shrugging, Dean replied with a childish grin, "Coin flip.

Ski slopes of Colorado or the beaches of California. California won."

"At least you put some serious thought into it," Shelby teased.

"Truth is, I was restless. I didn't feel anything was keeping me here, or I didn't want to think that there was. Either way, three days after graduation, I was packed and driving across the country," Dean said.

"Did you have a plan?"

"I did. I went to grad school, got into an internship program with a big company, and that's pretty much my story," Dean said.

"Do you like it out there in California?" Shelby asked.

"I do. The weather's great. I work. I surf. I travel. That's about all there is," Dean said.

"Parallel lives, minus the surfing. Work, kids, work," Shelby said.

"The kids part trumps my story," Dean grinned.

Shelby cocked her head, "You think so? Not sure I would have expected that from the consummate bachelor."

"Bachelor, yes. Consummate, not so much," Dean countered. "By circumstance, not by design."

"I see," Shelby said, sipping at her beer. Eyeing him for a moment, she smiled. "You aren't exactly as I pegged you when I first saw you at the restaurant."

Dean laughed, thinking about his experiences the day prior. Reality trumped expectations in nearly every instance. "Yeah, I've been learning things aren't always what you think from the surface."

Dean found the stroll back to the car considerably more comfortable and amicable than the walk to the restaurant. Shelby seemed to enjoy the evening stroll along the river and opened up enough to share a few childhood stories and about her children. She even accepted Dean opening her car door for her.

After a pleasant, open-air drive back towards the beach, they found themselves at the most awkward part of the evening-dropping Shelby off at her car. A look of anxiety and discomfort scribbled across her face.

Dean wrapped around the car and held the door for her. The pleasant comfort and easy conversation that embraced them at the dinner table and the journey to this point, suddenly melted away. Their sentences became forced and jumbled. Their mannerisms became clunky and robotic as though all of their muscles tensed. Shelby had a slight lean away from Dean as they walked.

Closing in on her parking space, Dean suddenly slowed his pace, stopping at the corner of Shelby's car. Allowing her to move a step beyond, protecting her space and minimizing the potential awkwardness of goodbye.

Spinning, Shelby faced Dean directly, relief and gratitude clearly expressed in her eyes. "Thank you. I had a nice time," Shelby said.

"I did, too."

"Goodnight," Shelby said and turned to her car, opening the door.

"Goodnight, Shelby," Dean said. He watched her for a moment, as if to ensure she was secure in her car. Spinning back toward his vehicle, he gave a quick wave as she pulled away.

Sitting back behind the wheel of his car, Dean covered his hands with his face and rubbed vigorously. With a deep breath, his mind whirled as he tried to reconcile the strange and intense feeling that was washing over him. A feeling that he had not experienced before.

Chapter Seventeen - Picnic on a Battleship

"Ahoy, there!" Cassie called from the top of the gangway. Waving her arm towards Dean, she welcomed him to join her aboard the retired *U.S.S. Battleship North Carolina*, the site of the Cape Fear Commercial company picnic.

Resting across the river from Wilmington's downtown, it served as a sentinel to service members from the boat's namesake. The naval vessel, stretching over seven hundred feet in length, was initially commissioned for World War II. It was converted into a museum and memorial.

"Well, what do you think?" Cassie grinned, her arms spread wide.

"I think I have not been here since prom," Dean admitted, admiring the ship. "Great place for a company picnic, though."

"We rotate sites each year. The kids love coming here,"

Cassie said, waving for him to follow. "Come on, I'll give the lay of the land."

Taking her lead, they walked along the wood deck to an archway that led to a wall of photos taken of Cape Fear Commercial employees and events throughout the year. "Families can take a tour at this station. It will take you all around the ship and share some of its tales. The kids have a couple of play areas up on deck." Heading to a rail, Cassie leaned over, "We have our games for later that will take place on the lawn, and at that dock, you can go on a jetboat ride. When you get hungry, there's food all day, but we will have a company-wide meal at twelve-sharp. You'll be sitting at Mr. Stevens' table up front."

"Sounds like you guys put on a great spread," Dean said.

"Ever since the first year it opened, the tradition carried on," Cassie nodded. Surveying the scene from their high perch, she offered, "Looks like everything is under control. You want to walk with me?"

"Sure," Dean agreed and followed her along the deck. The sun was coming down strong, but a soft breeze worked its way upriver, making the day tolerable.

Cassie tilted her head, a wicked grin crossing her lips, "Any more notches in that apology tour?"

Dean couldn't resist a return smile, glancing out at the water briefly, "No. No more apologies, so far."

"Well, the days young, we'll see what, or who, we can

conger up for you," Cassie teased.

"Let's hope I don't cross anyone else I feel that obligation to," Dean urged.

Cassie's eyes widened, "How did your dinner with Allie go?"

"You know, it was oddly...pleasant. Thomas is a great guy, and he's a thoughtful husband and father, I'm happy for Allie," Dean admitted.

"And, Allie?" Cassie's body wiggled a little as she emphasized her name.

"She's nice. Way nicer than I ever rated. I'd say she got what she deserved, and my nonsense didn't deter that," Dean said, shaking his head.

Cassie cocked her head, "But?"

"They're so welcoming and giving, both of them. I wish I could be a little more like them," Dean shrugged.

Sliding her arm around him, Cassie said, "Maybe you are a little closer than you think."

Dean laughed, "Not...even...close. But thank you."

"There's the woman of the hour," a voice boomed as they careened around the pilothouse of the battleship. "And it would appear her accomplice."

"Everything is tip-top. Guests are already checking in," Cassie reported.

"Good, good," Mr. Stevens said. "Dean, I would like to

introduce you to the most important person in my life, save for the Lord almighty. Mrs. Victoria Stevens. A woman with a heart of gold, and fortunately for me, horrible taste in men."

"Mrs. Stevens," Dean acknowledged, holding out his hand. "Dean Taylor."

"Ah, Mr. Taylor. Bart has told me so much about you," Mrs. Stevens said.

Dean wrinkled his nose, "Hopefully, some of it good."

Mrs. Stevens flashed a wry smile and winked, "Some of it."

"It's a pleasure, ma'am. I hope I can earn a rank of 'most of it' by the end of the day," Dean declared.

"He did tell me about the 'tour'. How is that going?" the woman asked, her question wringing in earnestness.

Dean shot Mr. Stevens a look while Cassie let out a snort.

Mr. Stevens shrugged, "The woman's like a CIA interrogator."

"Probably meant nothing to those I apologized to, but for me, it was a tremendous lesson in grace," Dean replied.

The response struck Mrs. Stevens well.

"That's a lesson well learned for most of us, dear," she smiled. Placing a hand on her husband's arms, she warned cheerily, "He's a charmer. Better watch yourself in your business dealings."

"We'll, uh, see you around, Dean. Enjoy yourself," Mr. Stevens gave a quick nod and escorted his wife to mingle with arriving employees and their families.

"Behind every good businessman...," Cassie grinned at Dean as she hooked her arm in his and continued their stroll.

As they walked, she would stop and introduce him to employees as they passed, including a few that he had met during their facility tours. Most would swap simple pleasantries and return to mingling with their coworkers or playing with their families.

A few would share how much Cape Fear Commercial meant to them, their family, or their town. One woman struck Dean, in particular. After their brief interlude, she placed a hand on his forearm, "If Mr. Stevens has to sell to someone, I'm glad it's to a young man as nice as you."

"Well," Dean gushed, "I represent a whole corporation."

"If you are their messenger, I'm quite sure we'll be fine," the woman said.

As she sauntered off and Cassie pulled him to the next group of families spilling into the picnic, he muttered, "More like your messenger to *them*."

"Ooh," Cassie squealed. "Mayor Jackson. Mayor of North Side."

Cassie introduced Dean to the mayor and his wife.

"Silly to be a mayor of a town of less than a thousand, it would seem, wouldn't it?" the mayor quipped.

"No, sir. Not if there are people you care about that need your services," Dean replied.

"Exactly! And as long as Cape Fear Commercial maintains

that facility like Mr. Stevens go gallantly has, the little town and her people will keep marching forward," the mayor said.

For most of the morning, Dean observed employees and their families interacting together. It seemed more like a giant family reunion than a company picnic. Mr. Stevens certainly was the center of attention. Most of the people seemed to revere him. It was more than a paycheck. He was a part of their and their families' lives.

The flow of arrivals yielded to a massive congregation moving through the offerings of the grounds and the battleship. Soon, a whistle from the grand naval vessel signaled it was time to assemble for lunch.

Mr. Stevens stood atop of the gangway as the employees and families looked up from the grounds. "I'll keep this short and sweet, as I'm sure a lot of you are like me- very much ready for lunch.

I just wanted to take a moment and thank all of you, all of the families that make up Cape Fear Commercial. This company makes stuff, sure. But what we are most proud of, are the people, the families that we get to support. You all mean so much to my family and me. And I love the clippings you send to Victoria and me. Whether it is Bobby Jenks making baseball all-stars, Jessie Briggs entering the Marines or Stan and Barbara Winwood welcoming their latest little family member, they all mean so much to us. Thank you.

"Okay. With that, let's grab the hand of someone close to you and say grace before we can all get to eatin'!"

Dean hung back with Cassie as the families stood in line to fill their plates with fried chicken, barbecue, and greens. Some kids skirted the long lunch lines and whetted their appetites with items from the dessert table.

"They really like him," Dean observed.

"They love him," Cassie said. "He loves them back."

"You don't see that very often," Dean remarked.

"Not exactly how things will run if Dana Holdings takes over?"

"Not exactly."

When the line dwindled to a few hearty appetites gathering seconds, Dean and Cassie grabbed their plates and made their way to their seats by the Stevenses'. Laying his plate down, Dean pulled Cassie's chair out for her. When she was seated, he took his own.

"Quite the party you guys throw," Dean remarked.

"It's nice being able to get everyone together. Especially those that work together but from different facilities. And the families," Mr. Stevens explained.

"Each site does things with their families throughout the year," Cassie added. "Started on their own accord. Now we help support them."

"I attend when I can," Mr. Stevens said.

"It's nice. You have been part of something extraordinary," Dean acknowledged.

"Yes, I have. *We* have," Mr. Stevens said. "I don't expect things will stay the same."

Dean shrugged, "You and your people have developed a culture, Mr. Stevens. I do not see that being undone with a shift in corporate heads."

"At least not right away," Mr. Stevens pressed.

"Yeah," Dean dropped his head and stirred the food on his plate.

When Dean looked up, his jaw dropped in recognition. He squirmed a little in his seat.

"Uh-oh, another apology coming?" Cassie teased.

Dean shot her a look, "Not exactly."

The individual Dean recognized was making a beeline up to their table. "Dean Taylor? No way!" a burly man bellowed.

Cassie sat back and watched the scene unfold.

The man rubbed his chin, "This guy busted my jaw in high school."

The Stevenses and Cassie looked surprised. Dean did know whether to run, protect himself or try to talk his way through the situation.

Seeing the looks amongst the table, the man waved them off and laughed, "No, no. I deserved it. I was picking on some scrawny kid, and he... he kinda set me straight."

Dean said calmly but cautiously, "Jake, it's good to see you."

"Yeah, man, you too. I want you to meet the better half and Jake Jr.," the man waved him across the table.

"Sure," Dean agreed, wiping his mouth with his napkin and setting it down on his finished plate. "Excuse me," he said as he stood up from his chair. He followed the big man who clapped him hard on the back with meaty hands.

Dean warily followed the man over to a table where employees and families of Cape Fear Commercial were busily feasting on their meals. As Dean closed in, his head dipped slightly in recognition of the woman sitting next to Jake's vacant seat. Subconsciously, he paused his gate for a moment.

Beaming with pride, Jake held an outstretched hand toward the woman, "I'm not sure if you remember Kayla, aka my bride…"

Dean choked his reply slightly, "Hi Kayla."

Kayla looked flustered for just a moment before Jake continued, "And this guy is Jake Jr. Don't know what I'd do without these guys and God himself. They turned my life around."

Dean waved at the three-year-old looking up from his corn on the cob.

"Jake, it looks like you've done well for yourself. You've got a great family," Dean said.

Jake looked at his wife and then back at Dean, "Did you two…"

"One date! We only went on one date," Kayla spat.

Frowning she muttered, "Not sure why only one, but..."

Dean smiled sheepishly at the man whose muscles rippled under his rolled-up sleeves, "What was that... junior year?"

Kayla nodded, "Yep. I think you took me to putt-putt golf on Long Beach. Jake and I caught up after the summer of our senior year, volunteering at a summer church camp. He hasn't been able to shake me since."

Jake swayed on his heels, his pride once more swelling, "You're stuck with me, Sweetheart."

"What do you do at Cape Fear Commercial, Jake?" Dean asked, really wanting to move the subject along.

"Security for the New Hanover facility. Like to work my way to head of security when old Hank retires," Jake replied.

Dean couldn't resist a chuckle at the man who somewhat resembled Paul Bunyan. "Look into taking a cybersecurity class or two online or at the community college, it will give you a leg up," Dean suggested.

"Cybersecurity?" Jake asked.

"Yeah, most people think of the physical aspect of security. You've clearly got that down. What they forget is the number of customer bank accounts that the company has stored is a huge liability for the company, more so than trespass. It could set you apart for the position," Dean said.

With a firm hand slapped on his back, enough to force Dean to lurch forward a step, Jake grinned, "Thank you, Dean. I'll do that."

"Don't mention it," Dean gasped, working his rotator cuff in a circle. "Well, I should let you guys finish your lunch. It's a pretty fun day here."

"Good to see you, pal," Jake said.

"Bye, Dean," Kayla called, wiping butter off of her son's chin. Dean gave her and Jake Jr. a wave goodbye.

Dean walked back to the head table. The lunch table lines had converted almost exclusively into dessert runs, plundering a sundry of pies and treats. Families headed off in the direction of tours of the battleship or games on the lawn.

Mr. Stevens saw Dean make his way over and sequestered him. The two walked the grounds together along the river.

"I wasn't sure about you when I first met you. If I couldn't trust you, I know I couldn't trust your company," Mr. Stevens opened up.

"Yes, sir," Dean nodded. "I wasn't thrilled with the delay of adding the facility tours, and even today, coming to the company picnic before we finished our deal. But I'm glad you had me do that. I would never have been able to humanize the numbers on the spreadsheet."

"And now?"

"No company can buy the exceptional people and culture that you have developed. No acquisition will keep a small town afloat without changing it," Dean said.

"And your company?"

"I put the language you requested into the contract," Dean said quickly.

"Good," Mr. Stevens nodded. He stopped for a moment and looked out onto the Cape Fear River.

Dean's eyes followed his briefly, lighting on the bank and the waters beyond the battleship. His mind danced with thoughts of the people as his eyes scanned the lively crowd. A group who had come together paused to hug one another as they connected. A toddler on a couple's heels suddenly raised her head, tracking a butterfly fluttering by. In a flash, the child was locked on the butterfly, following its erratic pattern across the lawn as it swerved, darting for the river.

Dean's first thought was the water itself. His second was the series of slides he spied along the river's edge. Without warning, he bolted from Mr. Stevens' side and sprinted toward the gap between the toddler and the water.

Looping an arm, he snatched the child up without breaking stride and refocused her towards her parents. Startled by the stranger's action, the child made a beeline for her parents.

He looked up and saw Mr. Stevens staring at him. Their eyes met, oscillated to the child, and then back to the river. At the side of one of the slides, just at the edge of a clump of pampas grass, was an alligator soaking in the afternoon sun.

Their eyes snapped back to one another. Dean rolled his

eyes and shrugged.

"I think I might post someone in this area, just to be safe," Mr. Stevens said, patting Dean on the shoulders.

"Good idea, sir," Dean replied, taking another glance at the gator, who seemed oblivious to the incident.

Dean manned the area until he returned with a volunteer to ensure that neither picnic-goers nor reptiles were molested. Satisfied that any new butterfly chasers were safe, they continued their walk.

He wasn't sure how the conversation arrived on the topic. It was one that Dean hadn't any intention to discuss with anyone. His confessed adoration of Shelby somehow made its way to the surface as he and Mr. Stevens walked. Dean could hardly believe his ears. He reasoned that the entire Stevens household shared the gift of interrogation.

Mr. Stevens looked thoughtful, "You should have brought her."

Dean looked dubious at the suggestion. "I don't think she would have come even if I had invited her."

"Never know if an invitation will be accepted until you extend it," abruptly Mr. Stevens cut off the conversation, "Well, it was nice talking. Good work with the kid. I've got to mingle. We'll catch up later." Without warning, he disappeared into the crowd.

Dean didn't know what to make of the CEO's sudden departure. Sitting on top of a dock rail, he settled in to lose himself watching the current of the Cape Fear River. He didn't know how long he had been soaking in the afternoon sun and eyeing the occasional wild inhabitant of the water or shoreline.

Tapped on the shoulder, he turned to find Cassie with a big grin on her face. "Mr. Stevens asked me to come get you."

Dean frowned, "Yeah, sure."

Hopping off of the dock railing, he followed Cassie up to the battleship gangway. Carving their way across the teak decking and through the families touring the boat, he found Mr. Stevens waiting for him. Cassie smiled at Dean and spun, walking away.

Dean looked at Mr. Stevens, who gave the simplest nod toward the bow. Confused, Dean saw a woman leaning against the rail, looking out toward the water. As Dean stepped forward, Mr. Stevens walked away in the same direction Cassie had.

"Shelby?" Dean called, incredulous.

The woman at the rail turned, her lips tight across her face.

"What are you doing here?" he asked.

"So, you *didn't* have anything to do with this?" she asked.

Dean shook his head and replied softly, "No."

"That's what Mr. Stevens said. He suggested I shouldn't be mad at you."

"And are you?"

"No. Not really," Shelby replied. "I mean, I am not usually kidnapped in the middle of a shift. With my boss' approval and obvious enjoyment, I might add."

Dean frowned, "Kidnapped?"

"If kidnapping means my boss lied that I was hired for a catering gig, picked up by a limousine, offered a glass of champagne and brought here, told to wait on the bow of a battleship, then yes. I was kidnapped," Shelby informed him. "That Mr. Stevens guy seems to like you. You seem to have mentioned me conversationally, it sounds. He took it upon himself to 'further our conversation' from last night."

Dean dipped his head, embarrassed.

"You truly had nothing to do with this; I take it."

"No," Dean shook his head.

"Well, I don't have a ride back to the restaurant. I guess I might as well make the best of it. Want to show me around this tub?" Shelby asked.

"I'd...I'd love to," Dean admitted.

Together, they walked the battleship. Following the tour route, they shared the experience while sharing light talk.

"Mr. Stevens tells me you saved yet another child. You aren't like a superhero or something. You sporting some tights under those pants or anything?" Shelby teased.

Dean laughed, "No, no tights. Today's rescue was nowhere near as imminently dangerous as yesterday's. Just redirecting a child to the safety of her parents."

"But an alligator? That sounds imminently dangerous," Shelby pressed.

"It wasn't really all that close," Dean rubbed the back of his neck.

"Al right. Play if off, hero," Shelby drawled.

In Dean's embarrassment, he mindlessly stepped through a narrow ship doorway at the same time as Shelby. The two were momentarily stuck against one another, staring at each other face to face for one electric instant before Dean wriggled backward, allowing Shelby to egress forward.

"Sorry," he bowed slightly.

"Mr. Unflappable, you seem positively...flapped?" Shelby declared. "I'm not sure that's how the words work, but..."

Dean offered her an annoyed glance but was welcomed by a warm grin in return. "If that's what it takes to see you smile, so be it."

"Ugh, don't you try and turn the tables on me," Shelby scolded. "This is all about you, buster!"

Together, they laughed as they explored the steel halls of the old warship. Winding their way through the maze of ladders and passageways, they were once again on the top deck. Shielding their eyes from the late day sun until they adjusted from the bowels of the ship. They found the festivities in the stages of winding down.

"That was fun," Shelby admitted.

"It was," Dean smiled.

"Well, I suppose I should find my chauffeur. The thing

probably turns into a pumpkin or something if I am not back in time," Shelby suggested, scanning the parking lot for the limousine that brought her there.

Dean pulled his keys from his pocket, "I could always drive you. I'd be heading that direction anyway."

Shelby looked unsettled for a mere moment before nodding, "Sure. That would be great."

As they approached the gangway, Dean held out his hand to help Shelby onto the metal walkway. Accepting, she slid her hand into his with a slight squeeze. Following her down, they found Mr. Stevens at the bottom, talking to his guests as they began preparing to go home.

"Ms. Shelby, perhaps next time, I'll simply send you a proper invitation," the CEO suggested.

"I'm glad you made me come, but if you insist on sending a limo again next time, it wouldn't be so bad," Shelby admitted.

"Dean, we'll see you Monday," Mr. Stevens said.

Dean reached out and shook his hand, "Thank you, sir. For everything."

"It's a pleasure," Mr. Steven assured. As Dean and Shelby walked on, he called out, "Dean, no apologies!"

Dean offered a subtle nod at the comment but continued without missing a step.

"Do you mind if I stop, real quick?" Shelby asked as they neared the gift shop and restroom area.

"Of course," Dean nodded. Leaning against the building, he watched the employees and their families begin to filter out of the park. He waved at several he had talked with over the past week.

"She's sweet, Dean," a voice called from the edge of the building. Cassie smiled at him. Walking up to him, she grabbed his hand. "Be careful. Your home is three thousand miles across the country. You're a signature away from going home."

"I know," Dean admitted. "It's not... We're just..."

"It's okay. Just, as a woman, as a friend, I am telling you, our hearts are different than yours." Letting go of his hand, she said, "See you Monday."

Dean nodded. Biting his lip, assuring her that he had heeded her warning.

Shelby came out, a little bounce in her step, "Ready?"

Dean looked at the southern beauty with Cassie's words ringing in his head. Accepting his hand, he walked Shelby to his car.

Chapter Eighteen - Evening Waves

Driving over the bridge towards downtown Wilmington, Shelby asked, "Would you mind *not* taking me back to my car just yet?"

"Sure," Dean looked over, "What would you…"

"There's a place I like to go. I don't get to often with the kids in tow," Shelby said. "Go right on Four-Twenty-One South and follow it until you can't go anymore."

Dean complied and swung the car south along the state route. Driving through Myrtle Grove and onto Carolina Beach, the evening drive was pleasant with the whoosh of air from the open-top cutting the heat and humidity of the day.

Crossing into Kure Beach, Dean glanced over at his passenger. To his delight, she seemed happy, almost content. It was a stark contrast to the air she wore during most of their encounters.

As instructed, he neared the end of the island and the last leg of the coastal road before leading into the ferry terminal. Dean looked over at Shelby, "You want me to cross over on the ferry?"

Shelby broke into a childlike grin and nodded her head.

"Alright," Dean replied, pulling the sports car into the cue. "You know, this is probably the last run of the night. We'll have to drive all the way around to get you back."

"I've got the time if you do. I was supposed to work all night," Shelby smiled.

Whatever was happening during what he knew had to be a brief interlude, he felt compelled to keep feeding her happiness. "Works for me," he replied.

They didn't have to wait long as the ferry docked, allowing the procession of cars to inch forward and onto the boat. Dean tried not to show his discomfort with the two-hundred-thousand-dollar rental car scraping up the ramp and maneuvering within inches of the other vehicles.

Finding their spot, Dean breathed a sigh of relief and turned off the car. Before he could speak, Shelby slapped his forearm with her hand, "Let's go up top!"

He chuckled at her exuberance, but certainly wasn't going to do anything to constrain her. Jumping out, he raced to her door. Both to beat her, forcing her to allow him to open it for her, but a little bit to place his legs between the door of the luxury car and any of the many obstacles that could befall it.

Dean reached for her hand as she stumbled up the steep metal steps in response to the jolt of the engines kicking into gear and pulling away from the dock. To Dean's surprise, she did not let go.

"Come on!" Shelby tugged at him. Scanning the deck, she found the spot she wanted and led him to the rail of the ferry. Leaning slightly over the edge, she drank in the air and misty salt spray kicked up from the bow and fed by the breeze.

"I love being on the water. I love looking at it and playing in it, but being on it…" Shelby breathed deeply. "Even the weird diesel-oil smell, it smells like life on the water."

"I like it too," Dean nodded.

"Thank you for this detour," Shelby said. "The girls enjoyed it the first few times I took them, but it lost its novelty on them. Cheap entertainment for a single mom while it lasted."

"Cheap not-a-date entertainment now," Dean grinned. He was surprised that Shelby leaned into him.

The breeze and spray kicked up, encouraging Shelby to burrow in closer. "I didn't expect I'd be chilly," she admitted.

Dean admitted to himself. He didn't mind at all. Putting his arm around her, his hand and forearm trying to shield her bare skin as much as he could.

Shelby didn't react. She just breathed content, and took in the experience of crossing the mouth of the Cape Fear River where it emptied into the Atlantic Ocean. Dean felt his heart dance around erratically in his chest, but remained still in their pose until the engines shifted as the tug turned toward the dock on the far side of the river.

The tiny town of Southport beckoned as the boat slowly churned toward its station. Passengers evacuated their spots on deck to head down to their cars. Dean and Shelby were the last remaining pair. Shelby's eyes fixed on the vista of the evening sky, integrating with the water.

"I suppose we should head down," she frowned, sounding.

With his arm around her, Dean steered her toward the bowels of the ferry and to the car. Following the cue, he gingerly guided the car down the ramp and onto the shore. Heading out of the ferry parking, they drove toward town.

In no hurry to head straight back to Wrightsville Beach, he took the harbor route along the water's edge of Southport. Shelby happily drank in the scene, "It's so quaint."

Noticing Dean bristle, just ever so slightly as they entered the town, she raised an eyebrow, "Is everything okay?"

"Yeah," he assured her. "Just not far from where I grew up."

"Show me!" Shelby squealed. Dean cast her an unsure glance. Pressing his lips tight as his mind raced, he reluctantly consented.

Driving through town, he pointed the car toward the outskirts and pulled off into a little community. Passing antebellum-style homes dotting the lane, he stopped in front of a modest house backed up to the Intracoastal Waterway.

"Is that it?" Shelby grabbed his forearm excitedly.

"That's it."

"It must have been nice growing up here," she mused as her eyes wandered, taking it all in.

"Yeah, I couldn't complain," Dean shrugged, looking lost at the house. Nearly two decades of memories fought for his attention.

Seeing a for sale sign posted in the front lawn, Shelby said, "We should check it out."

Dean frowned, "I don't know…"

"Come on. It will be fun," Shelby urged.

A thoughtful Dean sighed, putting the car in reverse. He rolled back far enough to nose into the drive. Parking in front of the house was a hauntingly familiar experience. He nearly expected his mother to pop out of the front door to greet them and to see his father tinkering on the boat in the back.

"Has it changed much?" Shelby asked.

"Less than I have, it would appear," Dean admitted.

Shelby danced up to the front windows, peering inside. By the time Dean had slowly ambled up, she was pulling on him to wrap around the house with him. Allowing himself to be led, they perched along the deck rail, looking over the sliver of backyard that spilled into the Intracoastal Waterway.

"What a grace place," she said admiringly. "Did you guys

have a boat?"

Dean nodded, "We did. I spent most weekends, at least when I was younger, tinkering with my dad on it. When it was right, the family would spend the day exploring every inlet between here and the end of Oak Island."

"I would love that," Shelby said dreamily, staring out at the water and following the coastline across the expanse.

"How about you? How was your childhood?"

"My daddy worked a lot. When he was home, we would play out on the Neuse River. Our version of a boat came with paddles, not a motor," Shelby admitted. "Most of the time, it was just Mom and me. She baked and sold cakes and treats to help make ends meet. We even won a blue ribbon at the Pickle Festival for our pickle pie."

Dean's face twisted, "Pickle pie?"

Shelby grinned, "Not as weird as it sounds. Never replaced any of the other recipes at the holiday table, but for the festival, it was pretty good. Mom thought the bourbon whipped cream made it, but Dad insisted on the candied bacon sprinkles."

"And you?"

"I kind of liked the candied bacon and whipped cream together, but not so much on the pie," Shelby shrugged.

"It sounds like you had a good childhood, too," Dean said.

"I did," Shelby nodded. "I'm trying my hardest to give the girls the best I can."

Looking down the waterway, she added softly, "It's tough."

Dean leaned against the rail, "I can only imagine."

Once more, Cassie's words resounded, warning him not to take this temporary situation too far.

Suddenly, Shelby's eyes glistened gleefully, "I *love* this time of the evening. Everything is cast in a bronze light, especially on the inland side of the island."

As she turned from the reflection in the house windows to take in the view direct, she spun straight into Dean. Instinctively, her arms reached out, landing on his. Tilting her head up ever so slightly, she looked deep into Dean's eyes. For a moment, they hovered breathless. As if drawn by gravity, they closed the distance between their lips meeting softly, each closing their eyes. The moment felt dangerous, electric, yet oddly comforting. Until it wasn't.

Shelby drew back, covering her mouth. Staring at Dean, her eyes told mixed stories. One version had her removing her hand and abandoning her thoughts for another kiss. The other screamed that she had just made a terrible mistake.

Rescuing her from her conflict, Dean suggested, "It's going to be dark soon. We should head up the road."

"Yeah," Shelby breathed in a hoarse whisper as she folded her arms and stared at the water.

Dean took several strides away down the porch, giving Shelby her space.

Her pain mortified him. Part of him wanted to rush back in, throw gas on the fire and see what catalytic explosion might ignite. The greater part of him just wanted to comfort her, be her friend. Let her know it would be okay.

Instead, he stood there, looking just past her. Still and silent.

Finally, Shelby breathed again. She turned to face Dean, "I am so sorry."

Dean shook his head, "Don't be. It was a serendipitous moment between friends."

"We're friends now, are we?" Shelby's punchy mood was returning.

Shrugging, Dean said. "Could be."

"That might be okay," she admitted. "I could use a friend."

"Good," Dean said, his tone steadfast. Brightening, he said, "Come on, one more stop, and I'll take you home."

Nodding, she followed him to the car. The air of begrudging acceptance to the assistance with the door had returned.

Firing up the convertible, Dean backed out of the drive and headed for the Brunswick County beaches. Turning east toward Caswell Beach, they watched waves splash just short of the highway as they sped down along the coastline.

Opposite of the beachside of the road, Dean pulled the car into a parking area. High above them, just in time to greet the bluish tones mixed with the pinks of the setting sun, the swirling light of the Oak Island Lighthouse came to life.

The sound of waves sang in harmony with the seabirds tweeting their stories to one another as they headed home after a day of foraging.

Shelby's eyes brightened as she looked up at the light, making its sweeping arch over North Carolina's southern tip. "This is wonderful!" she cooed.

Dean sat on the fender of the Aston Martin as he let Shelby take in the scene.

"The girls and I saw this from the ferry landing, but we never came all of the way here," she said.

"You'll have to bring them. You can climb all one hundred and thirty-one steps to the top and look out over their ocean kingdom," Dean said.

Shelby grinned, "I should do that."

Glancing at her watch, she said, "I want to explore, but…"

"We should head back," Dean nodded.

With an air to her voice, Shelby stood by the car, "Door, please, sir."

Dean laughed. Rolling his eyes, he opened the door for her.

As Dean whisked the car along the backroads following the curves of the Cape Fear River, the drive back to Wrightsville had returned to a comfortable affair. Dean and Shelby swapped stories from their lives, Dean learned more about her daughters.

When they found themselves back at the restaurant, parked alongside Shelby's car, there was hesitation in their movement. Hopping out of the car and jogging to her door, he found himself in an uncomfortable position. Parking right next to her, as she exited his vehicle, they were positioned directly in front of her driver's door. The two paused perilously close to one another, each bending backward as if there were an invisible object they were trying to avoid.

"Thank you, I had a nice time," Shelby said, then her head drooped, "Sorry about…"

Dean cut her off, "Forget about it. I genuinely enjoy spending time with you, for no other reason than— to enjoy being with you. That's it."

"No apologies, that's what your friend said, right?" Shelby said.

Knowing the misconstrued context, Dean simply nodded, looking at the ground as he did, "Yeah, that's right."

"Well, goodnight, Mr. Taylor. Thank you for a fun day and a wonderful evening."

"Goodnight, Shelby," Dean said softly, opening her door. He was happy to have the shield between them to avoid any rash impulses propelling them further together.

Looking intently into his eyes, Shelby sank into her car. With a quick smile at one another, Dean closed her door and took a step back.

Starting her car, Shelby backed out of her spot and drove away.

Dean's mind raced, filled with a wild, swirling surge of emotions. He watched her taillights disappear into the night. Fumbling with the keys to his car, he didn't want to retreat to his home. Not yet.

Swiveling his head, he searched for a path. Resting his eyes on the restaurant steps, he stole up to the double doors. They were pushed open, and he strode through, absently, he found himself at the bar. Ordering two bourbons, he washed one down in a single gulp. Slowly, he sipped the second, the whole time swirling the amber liquid in his glass while staring out at the night sky.

"Rough night?" the bartender asked, straightening up the bar in front of him.

"Not really... maybe, sort of. I don't know."

The bartender blinked. "One more?"

Dean looked at the glass he had just drained. Setting it on the bar, he shook his head, "No, I don't see how that's going to help."

Tossing a few bills on the counter, Dean slid out of his seat.

"Good luck to you, fella," the bartender offered.

"Thanks," Dean replied and headed back out of the restaurant.

Slipping behind the driver's seat, he dropped the top of the Aston Martin and put the car into gear. He drove south toward his rented beach house. As he approached the drive, he found himself keeping the throttle down and the wheels straight.

He passed right through Wrightsville Beach until he reached the very tip of the south end. Little entered his mind on his steadfast drive, and he enjoyed it. It was a sublime mental escape. When he reached the end of the road, he stopped the car at the edge of the way that paralleled the beach.

Getting out of the driver's seat, he laid on the hood, his hands behind his head resting on the windshield. He stared out past the Masonboro Inlet and the protected islands beyond. Off in the very distance, he could catch the strobing lighthouse beacon tirelessly making its cycle. Images of Shelby's look of wonderment as she stood at its base, her smiling in the passenger seat of his car, and the look in her eyes when his own were mere inches apart flashed with each passing beam.

Their kiss burned in his soul. It wasn't like anything he had felt before- no childish conquest or lustful impulse, something different. The kiss saturated his heart with a desire to do nothing other than to make that woman smile. To protect her sad heart and build a new wing. Letting her own her past and yet create a future in harmony with the other.

The words hit him as though he were having a conversation with himself. Shaking his thoughts, he rolled off of the sports car's hood and returned to the driver's seat. He headed home with more enthusiasm and awareness than he had when he mindlessly drifted south.

Chapter Nineteen - Storm Warning

Dean woke to slivers of blue light and pounding waves outside of his open beach house door. Opening his eyes all the way, he looked out at the Atlantic Ocean. Grey clouds were rolling in, fed by a breeze that was encouraging boisterous waves.

Kicking out of bed, he rubbed his face. Glancing at the clock, he knew he had plenty of time to shower and see if the coffee shop was open.

Running through his morning ritual, he jumped in his car and headed for the coffee shop. He was selfishly disheartened that it wasn't open but was happy for those who worked there that Sunday was a day of respite. Driving on, he crossed the bridge toward the Masonboro community on the outskirts of Wilmington.

Putting coffee as a waypoint en route to his destination, he found himself near the grocery store he had visited earlier in the week. Finding the coffee kiosk inside, he parked and went inside.

The store seemed busy for a Sunday morning.

"Tropical storm watch," the barista shrugged. "People are stocking up, but they never really hit here."

Nodding, Dean accepted his coffee, giving it a sip on his way out.

Firing up the car, he completed the drive to the destination. Seeing that he was early, he pressed on. Finding a little park along the water, he stopped the car and leaned back, enjoying his coffee while he watched the current lip into tiny whitecaps against the growing breeze.

Several boats cruised by as he watched. Glancing at his watch, he realized his early had turned into nearly late. Putting the car into gear, he accelerated hard, letting the tone of the dual exhaust declare his haste.

Quickly finding a parking spot, he jumped out of the car, grabbing his suit jacket in the same movement. Stretching it over his limbs as he walked, he snapped the lapels flat as he ascended the steps into the church. Nodding good morning to greeters on either side of the doors, he accepted the morning bulletin.

Scanning the lobby, he couldn't locate his target. Frustrated at himself for being himself late when he could have easily been early, it would have saved him from the uncomfortable search he found himself.

His eyes surveyed the pews after he poked his head into the sanctuary.

"Dean!," a sweet, southern voice called from behind him.

His heart skipped a beat as he spun, "Shelby?"

"What are you doing here?"

Dean started to speak before a woman waved vigorously from the front of the church toward him.

Shelby's head drooped visibly before Thomas Holmes joined the woman in the frantic waving.

"I'm meeting friends. Would you care to join us?" Dean asked.

Shelby hesitated for a moment and then shrugged. "I usually sit in the back, but okay."

Dean escorted her through the sanctuary to meet Allie and Thomas just as the pastor made his way to the pulpit. The worship band continued playing as he took his place in front of the congregation.

Dean and Shelby pardoned their way through the pew to take their seats next to Allie and Thomas. Dean shook Thomas' hand and waved a sheepish smile toward Allie, buried in attempting to decipher his connection with Shelby.

They were saved from further quizzical looks by the band winding down their song just as the pastor welcomed the church. As the pastor spoke on living a purposeful life on a Godly path, he suggested that the way God has in store for them might be different than the current path that they were on. Whether they were successful or not, whether they were good at or worked hard at something, it did not mean they were necessarily on the right path. That insight would need to come from reflection and prayer.

The pastor went further to suggest leading a successful life that was not God's intended use of your gifts would lead toward a less fulfilling life. Dean cast a glance at Allie and Thomas as the message resonated in his mind. He watched as Thomas nodded his head. To Dean, it seemed that Thomas felt he was on the right path and fulfilled.

When the service was over, the congregation milled about. Shelby excused herself.

"The kids would love to say hello to you. They were pretty excited that you were coming today," Allie said.

With a glance at Thomas, who was nodding in agreement, Dean complied, following them out of the sanctuary and down the hall to the children's wing. Standing in a cue to pick up Clarice and Ben, Thomas turned to Dean, "Why don't you come over for lunch? Nothing fancy, just dogs and burgers."

Dean was taken aback by the invitation, but struggled to find a reason why he couldn't. A part of him really enjoyed spending time with them. "Yeah, sure, that'd be great."

"Great!" Thomas said.

The family ahead of them received their child bringing Thomas and Allie to the front. They found Shelby standing to the side of the doorway, peering into the classroom. Four children were playing together as the children's ministry volunteer tried to round them up. Getting their attention, all four looked over to the doorway. Seeing their parents, they waved and raced over to the door.

"Mommy, Mommy, can Alena and Holt come over to play?" Clarice asked Allie.

Allie looked over at Shelby, who was collecting her children. "Why *don't* you guys come over for lunch? We were just talking about grilling hamburgers and hotdogs!"

"Well, I don't know…," Shelby reeled at the invitation.

"Can we Mommy? Can we?" both of Shelby's children sang in harmony.

Seeing Shelby's hesitation, Thomas added, "It's always so good to see kids who get along like that, especially Ben, who has struggled a bit."

Seeing both pairs of children stand arm-in-arm staring at their parents with hopeful smiles across their faces, Shelby relented, "Okay."

"Great, why don't you both just follow us from church?" Thomas suggested.

Shelby flinched at the word "both".

Suddenly, Ben and Clarice saw Dean and burst through the door to give him hugs.

Smiling, Dean reciprocated and, with a glance toward

Shelby, shrugged.

To Shelby's discomfort, Clarice spun to Holt and Alena, exclaiming, "This is Dean. He's a friend of my Mommy's and Daddy's."

"Hi guys," Dean waved.

"He's the man from the grocery store," Holt pointed at Dean.

Shelby's cheeks glowed red, embarrassed at the thought of the incident, "Yes, he's the man from the grocery store. Dean, these are my children, Alena and Holt."

"It's nice to see you again and actually to meet you," Dean said, bending closer to their level.

"So, it's settled. You'll all come over for lunch, and the kids will get to play," Thomas said, spinning for the exit.

Dumfounded, Dean, Shelby, and her kids followed the Holmes family out of the church and to the parking lot. Separating to their relative vehicles, they met at the church entrance and followed the Holmes' minivan.

As they arrived at the Holmes' house, the children quickly ran off into the backyard to play while Allie sequestered Shelby in the kitchen with her while Dean followed Thomas to the grill.

"How do you know Shelby and the kids?" Thomas asked and made neat rows of hamburger patties on one side of the grill and hot dogs on the other.

"Just chance meetings at a restaurant, a grocery store and a battleship," Dean shrugged, not wanting a big deal made of the pairing.

Thomas nodded though his brow wrinkled at the mention of a "battleship",' rolling the hot dogs in one sequential sweep of the tongs, he turned back to Dean.

"Do you two know her very well?" Dean asked, unable to mask his curiosity.

"Allie might. I've seen her and her children at church and church events. That's about it," Thomas admitted. "Seems nice. Keeps to herself as far as I can tell."

Dean peered through the sliding door, separating them and the women, nervously wondering what conversation they could be having. Little beads of sweat sprouted on his forehead.

Thomas turned to Dean, "Would you ask Allie for a platter?"

"Sure," Dean nodded. Wiping his brow, he slid open the sliding glass door. Seeing the ladies halt their conversation, both of their heads swinging in his direction made his heart tingle uncomfortably.

A polished smile swept his face, "Sorry to interrupt. Thomas was hoping for a platter?"

"Oh yes," Allie said. Disappearing behind the counter, she clattered through cookware.

Dean took the chance to shoot a smile at Shelby, who

flashed a half-smile, making him even more uneasy about the conversation the two were having.

"Here you go," Allie popped up with a metal tray in hand.

"Thank you," Dean said, accepting the tray. Making an awkward retreat, he returned to the backyard.

Helping Thomas collect the food from the grill, they were soon all gathered around the Holmes' dinner table. Hands stretched out along the table; Dean was awkwardly bridging Allie and Shelby. His hand with Shelby burned like fire. He wondered if she could tell and he hoped it was in his imagination. When the prayer was completed, the pair lingered just briefly before abruptly pulling their hands back their place settings in front of them.

In the same fashion, as they had the prior evening, Allie and Thomas quickly put their guests at ease. Engaging them in conversations about the kids, the pastor's sermon, and evening swapping a few innocuous stories from Allie and Dean's past as friends in college.

As they talked, Allie eyed the subtle interactions between Dean and Shelby. The slightest knowing grin creased her lips. When the meal ended, her eyes brightened, "How about we go for ice cream and a walk-through Airlie Gardens?"

Enjoying his time with both families, Dean said, "Yes, as long as I get to buy the ice cream."

"What do you say, Shelby?" Allie asked.

Looking at the children and their pleading eyes, she

relented, "Okay. Sounds good. I've always wanted to go to Airlie."

All four children burst into a chorus of glee, clapping their hands.

Shelby cut the celebration short, "But first, we need to help the Holmes' clean up from lunch!"

Her children jumped down from their seats and carried their plates to the counter. Dean followed suit, collecting Allie and Shelby's dishes along with his own.

Thomas was following his children to the kitchen with his plate. "You ladies relax, Dean, the kids, and I've got this!" Thomas called over his shoulder.

Dean and Thomas played with the kids and the soap bubbles as much as they used their efforts for cleaning. Despite their goofing off, they had the lunch dishes cleaned and condiments put away.

Gathering the troops, they followed very giggly children skipping their way to the driveway. Pausing, Allie announced loudly, "Our car will comfortably seat us and all of the kids. I suppose we could squish everyone together, or…Dean, you wouldn't mind driving Shelby while Thomas and I drove the kids, would you?"

Both Dean and Shelby started to speak, but Allie quickly whisked the kids inside the van, closing the door behind them. Grinning at her adult guests, she quipped, "Okay. See you there!"

Dean looked at Shelby and shrugged, "I guess it is you and

me, if you don't mind."

Shelby paused only for a moment before smiling, "I don't mind."

Opening the door for Shelby, Dean let her in and circled the car to his seat. Firing up the convertible, he followed the Holmes' van north to Airlie Gardens. Nearly seventy acres of gardens, lakes, and an explosion of azaleas beckoned them.

Piling out, the kids excitedly ran to the map at the end of the parking lot. Pointing out the areas they wanted to visit, their parents and Dean could hardly keep up. Starting with the nature trails, they skirted one of the large ponds that led to the Pergola Garden. Jutting out into the main lake, they walked to the very water's edge of the ornate stone cathedral, watching a pair of swans leisurely paddle along.

Dean smiled at the look on Shelby's face, the perfect picture of a radiant mother enjoying her children's excitement. Thomas squeezed Allie before snapping a photo of the kids along the water.

"Why don't I get your whole family?" Dean asked. Pulling his phone out, he lined up the Holmes against the stunning backdrop. Giving Shelby a look, she rolled her eyes before dropping to a knee and pulling her children in for a photo.

"You all look great!" Dean announced, admiring the picture he had just taken.

Site by site, the children urged their parents and Dean

along the park, from stopping to watch the trained border collie chase away geese to the butterfly sanctuary. As they passed rows of vibrant azaleas, they came to the five-hundred-year-old Airlie Oak tree. The children danced around the tree, playing and giggling together. Sitting on benches on either side of the lawn, the adults took a moment to let the children enjoy their time.

"You have great kids," Dean said as he sat next to Shelby.

"I'm a little sweet on them," Shelby replied.

"This has been a surprisingly amazing week," Dean admitted.

Shelby looked at Dean thoughtfully, "I might have to admit I have sort of enjoyed meeting you."

"Wow, I haven't had a review that glowing in quite some time," Dean laughed.

"A girl's got to be careful, you know," Shelby said defensively, a mischievous smile stretching across her lips.

Dean looked away for just a moment, his eyes catching how sweet Allie and Thomas were with one another. "Yes, they do," he admitted.

Holt and Ben raced by. Holt slammed on the brakes and called to his mother, "Hey, are we going to have ice cream?"

"Hey," Shelby teased back. "Maybe. Are you guys done playing?"

"I could eat ice cream," Ben said.

"Go ask your mom and dad if they are ready to go," Shelby

suggested.

Nodding, the boys darted off toward Thomas and Allie.

"I'm surprised we lasted this long," Shelby laughed, watching the boys having an animated discussion across the lawn.

Soon, they were racing towards the girls who were still playing by the grand, old tree. In moments, all four children were streaking toward their parents.

Joining back together, Thomas suggested, "We have a gift card for the ice cream shop. Why don't we just stop by, get the kids a cone and you two can catch up in forty-five minutes or so back at the house?"

Shelby reeled at the suggestion for a moment looking at her kids, at Dean and then back to Allie and Thomas.

"That's a great idea. The kids are having fun. You can walk to the Bradley Creek Pier. We didn't get there on the kid's whirlwind tour," Allie suggested.

"We'll be fine, *Mom*," Alena assured her mother.

"Oh, you will, will you?" Shelby huffed. "Fine, we'll be back at the Holmes' house in forty-five minutes."

The kids exploded into a chorus of cheers, and Thomas and Allie led the foursome toward their minivan.

As the Holmes' and Shelby's children disappeared, Shelby turned toward Dean, "Why do I get the feeling this was a setup?"

Dean shrugged, "Don't look at me, I'm as innocent as you are."

Shelby cast Dean an unsettled look, "Hmph. We might as well make the best of it."

Holding her arm out, Dean hooked his inside hers, and they strolled through the camellia-lined walk toward the pier. As they walked out on the dock, the breeze had picked up, and gray clouds had completely obscured the sun.

While others had abandoned the pier, Dean and Shelby had the wooden path over the water to themselves. Reaching the end, they leaned over the railing, shoulder to shoulder, taking in the scene of Bradley Creek cutting the series of islands between Wilmington and Wrightsville Beach.

Turning so that her hair was blowing away from her face, Shelby found herself staring directly at Dean. While that move was unintentional, wrapping her hands around Dean's neck and pulling him in for a kiss was very much intentional.

Dean's heart raced, feeling as though it might melt as it burned in his chest. Shelby's kiss set off fireworks in his head. Suddenly every concern in the world, every person had disappeared, and it was just the two of them on that pier.

Pulling away, breathless, Shelby didn't release the grip on his neck. Instead just stared into his eyes. Looking nervous, though defiant, she freed herself to the moment, to the man she shared the pier with, drawing in for another kiss.

Dean was unsure whether an eternity or a single moment had ticked by when their lips finally parted. Pulling her close, he wrapped his arms around her. Looking over her shoulder at the choppy water, he drank in the moment. He wasn't sure how, but he had genuine feelings for Shelby. He wasn't sure where the moment could lead, but in that snapshot of time, he didn't care. With a deep sigh, he realized that he, in fact, *did* care. If he was honest with himself, he cared quite a bit.

Shelby and Dean used every tick of the forty-five minutes allotted before they arrived back at the Holmes' doorstep. The breeze swirled, causing their patio windchimes to play an allegro tune as the string that tethered them strained to hold its grasp.

Dean thanked the Holmes' and said goodbye to Ben and Clarice. Walking Shelby and her children to her car, he gave Holt a high five, and Alena dove into his arms for a hug. "Thanks for letting me join you guys today," Dean said as they climbed into their seats.

At Shelby's door, they faced each other, staring deep into one another's eyes. Neither knowing precisely what to do or say. Shelby's arms fell to his. She wanted to pull him in for a kiss, but didn't dare.

Dean fought his impulses. Instead, he offered her a warm, earnest smile. Pulling her in, he gave her a quick hug and opened her door. Taking another opportunity to wave to the kids, he let her into the driver's seat. Their eyes asked a thousand questions that neither of their lips were prepared to answer.

"I had a nice afternoon," Dean finally admitted.

Shelby looked up from her seat and replied breathlessly, "Me too."

With a matching sigh, he closed her door and stepped away so that she could back down the drive. With a wave, he watched her, and the kids drive away down the street.

Suddenly aware that he was standing in his ex-girlfriend and her family's yard, he scampered to his vehicle. Starting the engine, he turned up the music and tried, as much as he could, to focus on the road instead of the searing thoughts of a shared moment on a lonely pier.

Dean placed the grocery bags on the counter of the beach house. Stocking up in case the storm hit as the news media had warned, he gathered enough items to get by. Tossing open the French doors to his patio, he listened to the surf pound as the breeze gave way to a legitimate wind.

Putting his groceries away, he poured a couple of drams of North Carolina Defiant whiskey into a glass and stood on his balcony. The beach had turned from a calming, welcoming picture to a dark and wicked scene. It dared anything in its path to face its wraith.

Leaning against the rail, he sipped his drink as he watched the evening grow ever darker, the waves crest higher, and the wind increase in intensity. The chaos of the incoming storm matched the swirling thoughts running through Dean's head. He'd enjoyed his time with Shelby. He loved seeing her smile. But he knew their time together would fade too soon.

The very next day, he was due to get a signature that would send him back home. Once he was gone, he didn't know when or if he would be back. He was developing real feelings for Shelby, but he knew it wasn't fair to either of them. It was better if she didn't know. They'd made a friendship, and that was the end of it. He wasn't sure he wanted it to be the end of it but couldn't understand how it could not be.

Closing his eyes as the wind battered him, drops of rain began to patter around him and dance off of the patio. He didn't care. He let the storm and the night overtake him.

Chapter Twenty -
Caught in the Storm

Dean woke to the sound of his phone alarm clock. Opening an eye, he saw the wind was still driving, though not as hard as it had during the night. Rolling out of bed, he rubbed his face. Staring out at the ocean, Dean watched as the tide crept just shy of the dunes, some waves splashing just over the top, trailing steams toward the beach house.

Wanting an early start to prepare for his meeting with Mr. Stevens, he got up to take a shower. Flipping on the bathroom lights, it was clear the storm had knocked out the power. A glance in the mirror, he tried to think if he could get away without showering. Rubbing his chin, he ran his fingers over his morning stubble.

He hoped the coffee shop or at least someplace in town closer to Cape Fear Commercial's headquarters might have power so that at least he could attempt to make himself presentable.

Dean began to pack- something that at the beginning of his trip, he couldn't wait to do. He now performed with great reservation. The weight of abandoning his revived relationships and his new ones alike was overbearing. He suddenly had trouble seeing California as home. Shaking his head, he felt as though a spell cast over him.

He decided he would leave his items at the house in the event the power came back on, and he could quickly get ready. Regardless, he planned on running back to the house one more time before taking off once he had papers in hand.

Grabbing his toiletry bag and his briefcase, he headed down the steps and to the car. Light rain continued to come down, tossed at a sharp angle from the still present wind. Though with each passing hour, the storm ratcheted down a notch.

Tossing his items in the passenger seat, Dean hit the start button and brought the sports car to life. Backing out of the stilt car park, he brought the car to the street and accelerated toward town.

Large puddles covered the road. The storm littered the streets with branches and blown debris. With the car's low-slung clearance, Dean had to dodge the obstacles as he passed. Coming up to a large portion of the road washed underwater, he slowed the convertible to a stop.

Seeing a small SUV trying to ford the puddle ahead of him,

he could see how deep it was, with water well above the doorsill. Sighing, he knew there was no chance the Aston Martin would make it through.

In the corner of his eye, he saw something wasn't right with the SUV, which suddenly pitched erratically. He realized what he was seeing. The vehicle had begun to float and was sliding its rear end off the road. Stopping and starting, it would spin and turn, slowly heading precariously toward Banks Channel separating the island from the mainland.

The SUV, momentarily stationary, Dean turned his emergency flashers on and tore off his suit jacket and his dress shirt. Tossing his phone and wallet in the car, he looked around for something, anything that he could use to try and reach the family. Spying a surfboard used as a decorative sign, he tore it off its moorings.

Unlatching a tow rope from the back of a boat in the adjacent parking lot, Dean quickly coiled it around his shoulder and ran full sprint toward the washed-out roadway. Jumping on the board, his momentum and the current rocketed him toward the SUV. He hoped whatever snagged the SUV kept its hold or they were all in huge trouble.

On the far end of the washout, Dean spied an emergency utility vehicle with its amber lights flashing inching as far as it dared into the wash. The SUV was coming up fast. Dean hoped his momentum wouldn't be the final straw, sending the family into the channel.

Spinning the surfboard sideways by planting his back foot hard, Dean tried to slow his speed to arrive at the vehicle with as soft a landing as he could. Motioning for the family to be still, Dean quickly fashioned a loop in the tow rope around the bumper and latched the carabiner to the SUV's tow hook.

With the tow rope between his shoulders, Dean dropped onto his belly and began to paddle across the current toward the utility vehicle. The driver of the truck saw Dean's rescue attempt and linked a tow rope of his own to bridge the gap. As Dean reached him, he began lashing the two lines together as he motioned for the man to get back in the cab and start inching backward as soon as he received the signal.

Feeling he had the knot as secure as it was going to get, Dean held his hand high and pointed toward the truck. The truck's engine cycled, pulling the lines taut. At first, the SUV didn't move. Dean feared the tow rope would snap as this exercise was well beyond its intended purpose.

The nose of the SUV snapped in the direction of the truck and, like a fish on a line, began to pull out of the water. The driver of the SUV revved the engine, desperately searching for the tires to bite on the pavement. Finally, the SUV lurched forward, creating slack in the line. The SUV surged forward until the tires were clearly in control, and both vehicles stopped.

The family scrambled out of the vehicle, visibly distraught

from their harrowing experience. While they collected themselves, the driver of the utility truck got out and shook Dean's hand.

"Man, I'm glad you came along," Dean said.

The man frowned, "What were you going to do if I didn't?"

"I was hoping to find an anchor point, and one by one, get the family out through it, or as many as I could before the SUV was whisked off into the channel," Dean shrugged.

"I'm glad it worked," the man said.

"Me too," Dean agreed.

The driver of the SUV strode forward. He was pale-faced and wide-eyed, "Thank God for you two. You saved our lives."

Dean knew the man was likely correct, but tried to put him at ease, "I'm sure it wouldn't have come to that, but I'm glad we were here to help."

"Y'all okay?" the driver of the truck asked the man as he scanned the family and their SUV.

"We're all pretty shook up, but yeah, we're okay," the father nodded.

"You might be best to avoid any puddles if you can't determine their depth and certainly any areas where the road is washed side to side," the utility driver suggested.

Nodding, the father agreed, "I won't be doing that again."

"I'm glad you're all okay, I guess I better get my own car to safety," Dean said nodding across the wash.

The utility driver looked concerned, "You need to be

careful crossing yourself."

Dean nodded, "I will. Mind leaving that line connected for a minute? If you park on the high side of the current, I can use it to propel me across."

The man looked at Dean for a moment and then seemed to understand. It was a technique for crossing rivers during rescues. Using a line in the current at an angle, would propel the swimmer to the other side.

Ensuring the family and their SUV were safe and on high ground, the utility driver positioned his truck as close to the ocean side of the road as he could. Letting the line out, he watched Dean hop atop the surfboard and glide a loose grip along the series of ropes until he was successfully across the other side. With a wave, he returned the surfboard in the vicinity of the shop's sign and hopped back in the Aston Martin. Firing up the heated seats, he maneuvered the car around and back toward the beach house.

Having shed his clothes and replaced them with dry ones, Dean set his dress shoes up to dry. Looking at his portfolio with an unsigned contract, he grabbed his phone. Dialing Mr. Stevens directly, he was met with the charming man's booming voice, "Dean, I hope you survived the storm okay out there."

"I did, sir. There's no power, though. I tried driving to the office, but the road is washed out between here and the bridge," Dean informed him.

"Well, no one is going to the office today. Sorry we didn't get the word out to you," Mr. Stevens said. "We'll have to mop up and see if we can't convene sometime tomorrow."

"Yes, sir," Dean agreed.

"Sit tight and stay dry," Mr. Stevens called into the phone. Dean didn't get into the fact that his advice was a little too late.

Hanging up, Dean reluctantly dialed his boss.

"You got the signature? That was quick work this morning," Marshall sang into the phone.

"I'm not sure if you saw the news. We got hit with a tropical storm. Powers out. Roadways are flooded. We're going to get together tomorrow," Dean said.

"This trip is dragging," Marshall said. "I was hoping to give the board good news at the monthly meeting."

"I was hoping the same," Dean admitted.

"I guess even you can't control the weather," Marshall conceded. "Stay and safe and bring that signature home tomorrow, Dean."

"Will do," Dean said and hug up the phone.

He paused for only a moment before dialing another number.

"Hello," a sweet southern voice called into the phone.

"I wanted to check on you and the kids. Are you doing okay?" Dean asked.

"We're fine. It was a wild night, but we survived. Lots of

board games in the candlelight with the kids," Shelby shared.

"You make weathering a storm sound...nice," Dean said.

"You control what you can. I wanted to keep the kids' minds off of it, snuggling together on the couch last night," Shelby said.

Dean paused, picturing the scene in his mind.

"It's good to hear your voice, I was worried about you out on the island," Shelby admitted.

"I'm pretty sure I have the wrong car to get through post-storm roads," Dean said. "Though in some spots, I don't think any vehicles are getting through right now."

"The kids and I were just about to head down to the church. The kids center is putting together kits for those who need it. I think Allie and Thomas were going, too. There is some post-storm flooding with the tides and the inland rain coming back down the rivers," Shelby said. "Too bad you're stranded. I was going to invite you over for a warm meal. It sounds like the island will be out of power for much of the day."

"That would be nice," Dean mused.

"Can I call you later?" Shelby asked.

"That would be great," Dean answered and hung up the phone. His mind churned as he stared at the waves rolling onshore.

Picking his phone back up, he made one more call.

As Dean slid into the minivan, he asked, "How're the roads?"

"Puddles and branches. Nothing like what you have back there," Thomas answered.

"Thanks for coming to get me," Dean said.

Thomas cast Dean a glance as he guided the van up the bridge, "I can't believe you waded through that just to volunteer to fill sandbags."

"Able-bodied," Dean shrugged, "With low tide, it was nearly as bad as it had been."

"We should get you back before high tide, I guess. Or better yet, have you crash with us," Thomas suggested.

"We'll see how the day goes," Dean nodded.

Pulling into the church parking lot, Thomas and Dean found a line of men filling sandbags, tying them, and stacking them in the back of several waiting pickup trucks. Without hesitation, they each took spots and got to work.

Dean manned the shovel while Thomas held and tied the bag before Dean hoisted the completed sand bag into the back of a truck while Thomas readied another bag. Repeating the process until the suspension of the pickup began to complain, that truck moved out, and another backed into position.

Completing several truckloads, Thomas and Dean hopped in the back of a laden pickup heading for a woman's house along Masonboro Loop. Her home was nestled close to a marsh fed by the creeks and streams of the channel. Jumping down, Dean and Thomas quickly went to work, placing bags along the most vulnerable portion of her yard, which threatened to reach the foundation of her home.

Eyeing their work, they felt the house was sufficiently protected. They jumped back in the bed of the truck to refill with more sandbags. Replicating their efforts with several more similar trips, they returned to the church wet, dirty and weary.

Thomas looked across at Dean as the pickup turned into the church parking lot for the final time. With a nod and smile, he reached across the bed of the truck and gave Dean a hearty handshake.

Hopping out of the truck, they joined several other men finishing their runs for the day. One of the wives waved them into the church. Following her, cups of water and lemonade greeted them along the hallway. The smells of cooked meat lured them into the large multi-purpose room.

The tables lining the room were filled with chafing dishes and serving trays. Women and children hugged their husbands and fathers. Their hosts ushered the work crew to wash up. Dean was intercepted by little arms wrapping around him. Looking down, he found Holt smiling up at him. Not far behind him were Alena and Shelby.

"I didn't expect to see you here," Shelby called.

Dean shrugged, "I had an unexpected day off."

"Wow, you really know how to relax," Shelby giggled.

"Strange as it may seem, I enjoyed myself out there. Hard work with outstanding men for some people that needed a hand," Dean said. "It was a great day."

"Dean Taylor, that almost sounded noble," Allie teased as she sent Thomas off to wash.

Clarice and Ben appeared behind her legs, "Hi, Dean!"

"Hi guys," Dean beamed. "It seems like you guys do some good things yourselves." Along the wall opposite of the table set out for eating, rows of care boxes lined the wall.

"We helped fill all of those boxes!" Clarice shared, her voice full of pride.

"You did good," Dean acknowledged.

"You're dirty," Ben said.

Dean took a moment to inspect himself. Clothes adorned with caked sand and hands to match, he suggested, "I suppose I am. Maybe I should wash up."

Heading to the men's room, Dean followed the suit of the other men. Cleaning his hands and splashing water on his face and neck, he tried to remove as much grime as he could. Walking back to the dining hall, he smiled to himself. He had indeed had a good day.

The Holmes' and Shelby, with her kids, were waiting for him, plates in hand. Alena handed one to him as he joined them.

The spread was impressive for short notice. A smorgasbord

of food was laid out, including a variety of meat, corn on the cobb, and refrigerator salads.

"Wow. How did all this come together?" he asked as they sat at a table together.

"Any family that was without power pulled whatever they feared would spoil if not cooked right away and voila a meal for a small army!" Allie shared.

"Well, I guess that makes sense. A delicious solution to a problem, for sure," Dean smiled.

"For sure!" Holt echoed, picking up a well-buttered corn on the cob.

Shelby looked at Dean, "I can't believe you left the island to do this."

Looking at the other men in the room, he frowned, "Nothing many other men didn't come out to do themselves."

"Yeah, but a lot of them came out for their neighbors, people that they knew," Shelby said.

"It felt like the right thing. I had a blast. We helped some lovely people out there," Dean said.

"Well, I'm glad you did. I didn't think I was going to be able to see you today," Shelby conceded.

Dean was happy to see her and the kids as well. With a secret sigh, he realized if the storm hadn't come, he could be on his way back to California. He was glad that he wasn't.

"I'm sorry it took a storm to get to spend time with

everyone today, but I am glad that I have the opportunity," Dean said.

Thomas looked at his watch, "It's high tide. I won't be able to get you back to the beach house tonight. You're welcome to stay with us. We don't have a guest bedroom, but the sofa isn't too bad."

"That'd be great," Dean nodded.

Clarice's eyes grew wide, "Can Alena and Holt come spend the night?"

Allie and Thomas looked at each other and then to Shelby, "It's okay with us...maybe play some family board games?"

Shelby hesitated, "Sure, why not."

"Why don't you come and visit as well?" Allie pressed.

Unconsciously, Shelby glanced at Dean and nodded, "That would be nice."

The Holmes' house was full of a festive air. The kids giggled with one another as Allie put on tea and cocoa. Gathering around the table, Dean found himself flanked by all four children as Thomas got the first games set up.

Shelby shot Dean a pleased look as he interacted with the children.

As Allie arrived with mugs in hand, they leaned over the table, collecting their cards. Playing one of the kid's favorite games, they played multiple rounds, trying to guess the spies by the secret cards they received.

After several rounds, Allie glanced at the clock. "Alright, my little spies, your next mission is to brush your teeth and get ready for bed. I think I'm going to be right behind you," she yawned.

Thomas ran up after the kids ensuring they were good.

"I am going to crash. Feel free to stay as long as you like or crash on the couch. I'll grab you some blankets just in case," Allie told Shelby. "Good night, Dean. "

"Good night, Allie. Thank you for everything," Dean said.

Allie cast a wicked grin, "You might be worth it."

"I'm going to go up and tuck in the kids. You want to join me?" Shelby asked.

Dean jumped out of his chair, "You bet."

Following Shelby upstairs, he joined the procession of parents hugging the children goodnight.

"Mr. Dean, I like you," a sleepy Ben said, his arms around Dean's neck. "I like you too, buddy. I like all of you, little critters."

"Goodnight, Dean," Alena and Clarice chorused.

"Goodnight, girls."

"Mr. Dean," Holt said, a look of worry across his face. "Are you staying here tonight?"

Dean nodded, "I am."

"Good," Holt smiled and sunk into his pillow.

Dean walked past the parents as they gave their children

one last look before turning off the light.

"Goodnight, you two," Thomas whispered, his arm around his wife.

"Goodnight, guys!" Dean and Shelby whispered back.

Quietly descending the steps, Dean and Thomas walked to the sofa opposite the gas fireplace that Thomas had turned on with their wet shoes drying in front of it. Grabbing a blanket, Shelby plopped down, patting the spot next to her. Happily complying, Dean settled in next to her.

Shelby leaned close to him, resting her head on his shoulder. Reaching his arm out, he pulled her tight.

With a deep breath, Shelby said, "I kind of like this."

"I kind of do too," Dean whispered back.

"What do we do about it?" Shelby asked in a breathy whisper looking up at Dean.

"Enjoy every moment that we have together," Dean replied.

Shelby pushed her head forward. Dean followed suit until his lips met hers, soft and sweet. Eyes closed, they pressed even closer, absorbing their connection to its fullest.

Dean had no concept of how long they had been like that. He didn't care. The flicker of the flames in the gas fireplace caused Shelby's eyes to shine. He wanted to pour himself into them. Unable to resist, he kissed her again.

"The kids like you," Shelby whispered.

"I like them too."

Shelby stared at the man next to her. "I didn't think I could feel…anything like this again."

Dean stared at her, her brilliant eyes, her freckles, her sweet smile. She was such a contrast to the bitter, distant woman he had met at the restaurant hardly a week ago. His heart nearly leaped out of his chest.

Leaning his forehead against hers, he gently caressed her chin. Their eyes hovered inches from each other. They were so close that their breath, their heartbeats began to match, working in perfect rhythm with one another.

"I could stay here all night," Shelby cooed.

"I don't happen to be going anywhere," Dean said.

Snuggling on the couch, they slept sitting next to one another, Shelby's head on Dean's shoulder through the night.

Chapter Twenty-One - Clean Up and Clear Consciences

Dean awoke, slightly startled as he was sitting up in an environment, not his own. As his eyes began to focus, so did his mind. Nestled into his shoulder was a sleeping beauty.

With a smile, Dean gently squeezed her close. He remained still for nearly an hour before the pitter-patter of little feet descending the stairs alerted him that at least a couple of the children were up. Nudging Shelby slightly, she woke, sleepy eyes batting the world into view as two smiling boys stood in front of the sofa.

"Good morning, boys," Shelby sang sleepily.

"Hi, Mr. Dean," the boys chorused.

"Good morning. You guys sleep well?" Dean asked, to the pair of nodding heads.

Heavier footfalls descended the steps. "Boys," Thomas

called.

The two heads whipped up toward the stairs. "Good morning, Daddy," a sheepish Ben called softly.

"What say I pour some cereal for you two and make some coffee for the rest of us?" Thomas suggested.

Nodding, the boys streaked to the kitchen, following Thomas.

"Good morning," Dean smiled at the face staring up at him.

"Good morning," Shelby purred, burrowing herself against him.

Looking up, Shelby planted a kiss on Dean's lips before pulling away as more feet scampered down the steps. Counting two pairs of feet, she called, "Good morning, girls!"

"Good morning, Mommy!" "Good morning, Ms. James!"

The scent of coffee began drifting toward the living room. "Coffee?" Dean asked.

Shelby's eyes widened, "I would *love* that!"

Dean wriggled out from the blanket and followed the scent of coffee into the kitchen, where the boys were busily munching on bowls of colorful cereal.

"Coffee?" Thomas asked cheerily.

Dean nodded.

Thomas pulled out two mugs and filled them with coffee.

"Milk or sugar?" Thomas asked.

Dean suddenly realized how little he knew about the alluring, sweet woman in the next room. Leaning into the living room, he asked, "Milk and sugar?"

"Yes, please," Shelby nodded sleepily.

Dean disappeared and reported to Thomas.

As he walked toward the living, he spotted a sheepish Allie who was yawning her way down the stairs. "Coffee?" Shaking his head, he snapped his fingers, "Right, still a Pepsi girl?"

Allie grinned, "Still a Pepsi girl."

"Got it right here, hon!" Thomas called from the kitchen.

"One of the many reasons why I love you, Thomas!"

Dean laughed, "You've got a good man, there."

Allie looked at Dean square in the eyes, "I do."

Spinning, Dean continued his trek to the living room sofa. Dean handed Shelby a coffee, eliciting her to purr, "Thank you."

Sitting next to her, they drank their coffees in silence, allowing the warm liquid to work its way into their weary bodies. As they leaned into one another, Thomas came into the room reading off of his phone.

"The church is doing repairs for people around town today. Care to help?"

Dean looked thoughtful for a moment before nodding, "Yeah. Yes, I would."

"Great. We'll head out after breakfast. Yogurt and granola, okay?" Thomas asked.

Dean nodded.

"Is it a family affair or guys only?" Shelby asked.

"All hands," Thomas replied.

She got up, her hands cupped around her mug, "What do you think kids? Up for a little more helping people today?"

"Are Clarice and Ben going?"

"They are," Allie replied.

"Yay!" Shelby's children cheered.

Stepping away, Dean dialed Mr. Stevens.

"Hullo…," Stevens' voice rang through the phone.

"Mr. Stevens, I hope you weathered the storm okay," Dean said.

"I did, I was more concerned about you," the CEO stated.

Dean said, "I'm fine. Thank you. I know we missed yesterday's meeting, and we were going to look at today. If it is okay, I wanted to see if we could push out one more day. I was hoping to work with a church group today, helping people clean up and restore after the storm."

"That certainly sounds more important than a business meeting, at least in my book," Mr. Stevens agreed. "Catch up later this afternoon on resetting plans?"

"Thank you, sir. I'll look forward to it," Dean replied into the phone.

Staring at his phone, he looked at the urgent text from his boss. With a deep sigh, he hit the call button.

"Dean, what's the news? You at the airport heading back?" Marshall's voice rang through the phone.

"No, sir," Dean said. "With the storm, most of the people's lives around here were turned upside down a bit."

"You don't need the people. You need one person with a pen in their hand. Come on, Dean. Now is a great time to get a signature while they have other things to worry about," Marshall instructed.

"Mr. Stevens and I are due to connect later this afternoon to reschedule the final signing tomorrow, and then I'll be done," Dean stated.

"Are you keeping up with your other accounts? I didn't see anything come through from you yesterday," Mr. Stevens said.

"I didn't have power yesterday or internet, so no," Dean said. "Today, I was hoping to volunteer, helping the town get back on its feet."

"I don't pay you to do that," Marshall spat. "I pay you to close deals, jump back on a plane, and get ready for the next deal."

"Consider it a vacation day, then sir," Dean said flatly.

Silence overtook the phone for several long moments. "Dean, I don't need to remind you that this deal, this extended trip into your childhood past, which we are paying for, has your promotion hanging in the balance. And I've got to tell you. It's looking very tenuous at the moment."

"I understand, Marshall. I'll get this done. I'll be on a plane tomorrow afternoon," Dean assured him.

"You had better be." The phone went dead.

Dean stared at his phone before shoving it in his pocket. His conversation-soured mood was quickly turned around by four children bursting into the room followed by Shelby.

"Everything okay?" she asked.

"Yeah, just work stuff," Dean replied. "Are we ready to go?"

"I think so, you can ride with me, and the kids and Allie and Thomas can catch up," Shelby said. "Clarice, let your mom and dad know we're taking you to the church and will see them there, okay? We'll start loading the car."

"Speaking of cars…and clean clothes, would you mind running by the beach house?" Dean asked.

Clarice ran off to tell her parents while Shelby escorted the rest of the kids toward the car. Finding a seat for everyone, Shelby got them settled by the time Clarice streaked out and jumped into the last vacant spot.

Arriving at the church, Dean pulled in next to Shelby as they joined several other families coming to help. A man with a clipboard started cataloging the assembled helpers and matched them with assignments. Seeing them arrive, the coordinator made a note and motioned for them to gather near another man who was sorting tools into the bed of a truck.

Dean introduced himself with an outstretched hand.

"Davis Coleman," the man replied, giving Dean a shake. "Know anything about roofing?"

"Only that I know I shouldn't fall off. I can haul stuff and drive nails," Dean offered.

"Works for me," Davis said. Sizing up the other helpers, he added, "This will do. The house we're going to has a couple of younger kids. They might like the company."

Thomas and Allie pulled up and joined them to receive instructions. In short order, they had piled back in their vehicles and were following the man with the truck.

They arrived at a street that seemed particularly hard hit by the storm, though the age of the homes likely had a factor in the hand the surge dealt them. Another group from the church had pulled up at a house a few doors down.

Pouring out of their vehicles, they stood on the curb as Shelby and Allie walked up to knock on the door. David stood back, surveying the house as best as he could. A patch of missing roof shingles was evident.

"*There's* your problem," Davis quipped as he studied the house.

A woman opened the door, surprised to see Allie and Shelby and, even more, surprised to see a crew gathered on her front lawn. Two little faces pressed out from behind her.

"Ma'am, my friends and I are with Harbor Light Church. We heard your house got a little beat up from the storm. We have tools and supplies and wanted to see if we couldn't do some mending for you," Allie asked.

The woman looked confused for a moment. She was suspicious of the crew's intent.

"We're just neighbors being neighborly," Shelby added.

"Well, the world could always use a little more of that," the woman admitted. "I'm Stacy. These are my kids Stevie and Jackson."

"I'm Allie and this Shelby. Those are our kids over there," Allie waved the kids over and introduced them.

"Them boys need anything out there?" the woman asked, looking at Davis, Dean, and Thomas.

"No, ma'am, I think they brought everything that they need," Shelby answered.

"Alright, well, come in. I'll fix up some tea," Stacy said.

Receiving a thumbs up, the men quickly went to work. Their first task was piling the windswept debris on the lawn and strewn roofing by the curb so that they could work safely. Setting up ladders, Davis instructed Dean and Thomas on what they could carry over and put everyone in a position to begin securing the family's roof.

Thomas worked on reinstalling a gutter panel that had been hit by a branch and was dangling from the eaves while Dean hoisted shingles over his shoulder and climbed the ladder, tossing them on the roof where Davis began installing them.

Noticing the fence gate had been blown off of a hinge, with the family's dog taking great interest in it, Dean decided to tackle it in between hauling supplies for Davis. Stripping the suspect hinge down, Dean reaffixed it to a healthier piece of wood and larger screws.

Job one completed, he found Thomas and Davis finishing with their projects. Davis inspected the rest of the property. Satisfied his crew met the house's immediate needs, he called the church coordinator to have the designated clean-up truck pick up the debris and receive instructions for their next stop.

Collecting Shelby, Allie, and the children, they piled back into their cars and headed to their next site. They soon found themselves in a retirement community of mobile homes. The storm had ravaged the entire neighborhood. Tree limbs turned the roads into obstacle courses along with clogged drains, which left standing water that leached into the adjacent lawns. The worst were the homes themselves, which had missing siding, sagging porch roofs, and were covered in tree branches.

Davis tackled the most severe construction projects leaving the rest of the contingent to start pouring over the additional needs. Dean worked on the large tree limbs while Thomas tried to unclog the storm drains. Shelby, Allie, and the kids cleaned up smaller debris and reset outdoor furniture, flower boxes, and lawn ornaments.

Working through the day, joined by reinforcements from

the church, they steadily returned the neighborhood to order. Capable gentlemen came to help while ladies tended to their battered flowers. Others appeared with coffee, tea, and cookies. At one point, several ladies and their husbands set up tables in a driveway and set out sandwiches and iced tea.

Beckoning the workers over, urging them to put down their tools, the neighborhood and church volunteers gathered around the folding tables. Linking together, they prayed for the food, for the survivors of the storm, and for God's grace delivered through the volunteers.

Cleaning up, the volunteers sat with the residents, getting to know one another and sharing stories. Sandwiched between Shelby and an elderly couple, Dean enjoyed swapping tales about life in the Carolinas and storms that they had endured throughout the years. Dean learned the man, a veteran, used to work for Cape Fear Commercial. The man shared how good they had been to him, even as he entered retirement.

When the crew finished their meal, Dean shook the man's hand and thanked him for the conversation. With a hand on Shelby's back, he helped her usher the kids to Davis, who was reviewing the next round of duties. Working side by side with Shelby and the kids, they continued to make good things happen in the neighborhood.

The sense of community, the hard work, and the good deeds for good people filled Dean's heart with a feeling of contentment. Working alongside Shelby was magically. Occasionally grins and captured glances would send him over the moon. Despite the context of what they were doing, cleaning up muddy tree limbs and blown refuse, it was one of his favorite days that he could recall.

The crew worked deep into the afternoon and were surprised when a Lincoln SUV, followed by several additional vehicles pulled into the mobile home park. They even more surprised when Mr. Stevens, his son Chester, his advisor Jacob and finally Cassie got out of their vehicles and walked toward Dean in the middle of the street.

Shelby, Allie, and Thomas stopped what they were doing and observed the impromptu meeting. Dean leaned on the long-handled shovel he was using. Removing his glove, he shook Mr. Stevens' hand.

With a confused bend in his brow, Dean asked, "What... What are you doing here?"

Mr. Stevens smiled, "A little bird told me some Californian was here doing good deeds. I figured it might be you."

Dean cocked his head, "A former Carolinian with his friends."

"I see that," Mr. Stevens waved a hello to the small crowd that had loosely gathered a few steps from their conversation.

With a breath, the Cape Fear Commercial CEO reached

into his breast pocket and pulled out a folded set of papers. Holding the documents in front of him, Mr. Stevens explained, "I like what I have observed, what I have heard since you first presented in my conference room. The more my team and I have gotten to know you, the more I have come to like...and trust."

Waving the papers, he continued, "I have signed the agreement to allow Dan Holdings to acquire Cape Fear Commercial. There is one conditional addendum I had my attorney add to the base document, however."

Dean shot Mr. Stevens and the document a wary look.

"I want you to stay on as the managing executive between the two entities. In that, I am assured that Cape Fear Commercial and all of the people that make up its heart and soul would be taken care of in the transition and the future," Stevens declared. Handing the papers to Dean, he urged, "All we need is your signature to make it official, and we can proceed with the rest of the legal mumbo jumbo."

Slowly, Dean reached for the papers. Mr. Stevens produced a pen from his opposite pocket and handed it to him. Dean couldn't hide his contemplative, concerned expression.

Mr. Stevens studied his hesitation intently.

The crowd, especially Shelby and Allie felt the electricity in the air over the exchange.

Dean stammered as he absently tapped at the papers. Looking directly into Mr. Stevens eyes, he swallowed hard as he said, "Sir, I appreciate your offer…and your faith in me. But my life, it's no longer here. Not in North Carolina."

"Isn't it?" Stevens pressed, an eyebrow raised.

Looking at Shelby, Allie and Cassie then back to Mr. Stevens, he said, "No, sir. I'm sorry, I have to go back to California. It has been wonderful to meet you. To spend time with you and all of the people that make up Cape Fear Commercial. Spending time with others, and their families… but no, my home now is in California." He admitted begrudgingly, almost as much to himself.

Mr. Stevens patiently waited for Dean to gather himself and finish his thoughts.

"Coming back here has woken me up to so many things about life…about myself," Dean turned toward Allie and Thomas, and then toward Cassie, "It taught me about good people, and grace and friendship."

Panning toward Cassie, he added, "It reminded me about a part of my life I had left behind and buried. People and memories that deserve to be cherished as a good part of me."

He turned toward Shelby, who wore a pained expression on her face, "It showed me things I had never experienced before or thought were possible."

"But Mr. Stevens, I'd love to accept your offer, I just can't," Dean defended.

The CEO was disappointed but thoughtful and measured

in his response, "I see."

With a nod toward the papers, Mr. Stevens asked pointedly, "Can you promise me, promise all of the people that you had the opportunity to meet at the facilities, at the picnic that their roles, their lives will remain intact if we complete this sale?"

Dejected, Dean dropped his head, "No, sir. I cannot promise that. Not after the prohibition period expired. In fact, I would be surprised if Dana Holdings, or any other venture buyer, wouldn't impose major changes within the first two years following the signing of this contract. Northside, Holly Vale..." Dean shook his head slowly.

"Hmm," Mr. Stevens stared directly at Dean, "I appreciate your candor, Mr. Taylor."

Without another word, Dean handed the pen and documents back to Mr. Stevens. He looked at the man as though a child would when they disappointed a parent.

Mr. Stevens shot a quizzical glance, "Can I ask what becomes of you if you return empty-handed?"

Dean shrugged, "I lose my shot at becoming a principal at Dana Holdings, at least for now. But, I wouldn't say I will be heading back empty-handed." Again, looking at Cassie, Allie, Thomas, and Shelby before finally returning to Mr. Stevens. "This trip has left far from empty-handed."

"Very well. I am sorry we won't be working together. I think we might have made a good team. Farewell, Mr. Taylor,"

Mr. Stevens declared, extending his hand towards Dean.

Shaking his hand, Dean admitted softly, "I'm sorry as well. I wish you luck, too, sir."

Mr. Stevens nodded. Spinning, he walked away from Dean, his entourage in pursuit. Cassie stayed behind for a moment.

She wore a mixed visage, which ultimately melted into a warm smile, "You did the right thing."

Dean cocked his head, "It somehow doesn't feel that way."

"It's not always about what people want to hear so that they can feel good about the moment. It's about being honest with the moment. You could have inked that deal, and you know it," Cassie said.

"No," Dean shook his head. "No, I couldn't."

"See, it's like the Dean I knew all grown up," Cassie gave him a teasing grin. Softening, she extended her arms, hugging him. "It has been nice to see you. Stay in touch this time, okay?"

Dean hugged her back. "It was nice to see you too. Thank you for everything."

"Isn't it nice?" she asked as she pulled away to catch up with her boss.

"What do you mean?"

"Even when the truth is difficult for people to hear, you get to walk away without apologies," Cassie said. With that, Cassie scampered to catch up with Mr. Stevens.

In her wake, Dean realized a silent crowd had gathered to witness the exchange. Sheepishly, he said in a matter-of-fact tone, "Well, I guess we should get back to it, huh?"

Hoisting the shovel, he turned toward the audience, ready to move to the next neighborhood task.

Shelby strode forward, tears welling up in her eyes. Her freckled cheekbones levied directly in front of him. Grabbing the shovel handle away, she said, "It's okay, Dean. *We've* got it. You have a life, your *own* life to get back to in California."

Dean starts to protest, his jaw dropped open, ready to speak, but the sharp look from Shelby stopped him cold. Without a word, Shelby spun and defiantly walked away, shovel in hand. Gathering Holt and Alena, she walked steadily toward the far end of the neighborhood.

Dean could do nothing but stand in the middle of the street and watch them walk away. His heart was falling into the acidic pit of his stomach.

Allie moved from the crowd and squared up in front of him. With a kind smile, she placed a hand on his chest and offered, "You are a good man, Dean. The choices you make are your own. The rest of us don't have to necessarily like your path or join you on it. But when you are honest with us, we get to support you on it. We make our choices whether or not to let you into our lives, our families, our hearts. Trust that you will be there, whether or not you actually are."

She swallowed hard, giving him a warm hug, "It was good to see you. Keep going to church. It's good for you. And stay in touch."

"You are amazing. I'm so grateful to have caught up with you...and Thomas. You have a great life, wonderful children. I'll stay in touch," Dean promised, releasing her.

Thomas stood behind his wife and stepped forward as she went to stand by her children.

Dean reached out to shake Thomas' hand. He was surprised when he instead received a hearty sideways man hug. "Good luck, Dean. We appreciate all that you did for our community while you were here. I hope we will see you again."

"You will," Dean promised. Waving toward the kids, he subconsciously scanned the crowd. In the back of his mind, he knew what or rather who he was looking for. He also knew that someone was gone. Dejected, he nodded toward the crowd of volunteers and began his walk away from the work crew.

He was surprised to see Cassie leaning against his car, waiting for him.

She offered him a sideways grin, "I was curious."

"Curious?" Dean frowned.

"Curious if it that was really it. Your final decision. Just pack up and head home?"

Dean shrugged, "What else am I supposed to do? I left Wilmington over ten years ago. I have to get back to my home, my life."

"You *did* come back home, Dean," Cassie says sharply. "You have a life. It's right here. Your friends. Shelby…"

Dean bit his lip. Staring off in the distance, he felt as though eyes from the work crew were staring him down. He was sad and disappointed but couldn't put a finger on it. What he wanted at that moment was to get away. Snapping back, he said curtly, "It's been good to catch up. You should come out west sometime. If you do, look me up."

Cassie stared at Dean, clearly dissatisfied with their conversation, "Yeah, if I ever do."

Reluctantly, she watched Dean climb into his car.

Jumping into the Aston Martin had never felt as ostentatious as did at that very moment. Much of the congregation stopped to watch him. The car growled to life, fueling the attention he was receiving. Putting the luxury car into gear, he turned the wheel and sped away.

Subconsciously, he glanced in his rearview mirror. Pressing the throttle, he distanced himself from those anchored in the coastal Carolina town.

Chapter Twenty-Two - Welcome Home...?

Dean walked through LAX. The overwhelming mass of people scurrying through the airport terminals made his head spin. He was barely aware of any one individual, but keenly conscious of the volume of people jostling by.

The noise and chaos welcomed him back to California. Leaving the bustle of LAX, the dense traffic quickly consumed Dean. Cars merged, sped up, and braked to get ahead, only to fall back again. So many people, all oblivious to the lives right next to them.

Reaching his condo, he tossed his keys on the hall table just inside the foyer. Dropping his bags on the floor, he walked to the end of his small space and flung open the sliding glass doors leading to his narrow balcony. Looking over the bumper to bumper traffic of the Pacific Coast Highway, he studied the beach.

The low rolling waves rattled against the shore. The beach itself was dotted with people as far as the eye could see—the boardwalk stringing along the beach even more so.

Watching the people interact, he put himself down along the boardwalk in one of the many watering holes he and his friend would frequent. The same scene would play out. Everyone in their highest polish, was competing with the vast numbers of equally outwardly appealing people also trying to command attention.

Dean's own experiences in those very beach side bars were just that– aesthetically pleasing but hollow. Not that depth couldn't be found. It was just rarely accessible and reached amidst the frenzy of the rat race.

Dean flopped on his bed. His mind reeled like a projector on fast-forward, clips flashing in his mind one after another. He laughed at himself. He was so adamant about coming home as soon as humanly possible, but now that he was there, home was the furthest from the feeling that had encompassed him.

He tried shaking his head as though his adventures in North Carolina over the past week were merely messing with his mind.

Thoughts of Cassie, Allie, and Thomas consumed him. The grace, hospitality, and kindness they afforded him, though he did not feel as though he deserved a bit of it. He was grateful that after all of this time, he could call them friends.

Mostly, he thought of Shelby and her children. The last

thing he wanted to do was hurt her, but that was precisely what he did. It stung him in a similar fashion as when he had hurt Allie and carried that weight with him for the better part of a decade. He fought to earn their trust. The moment he had that trust in his hands, he let them down, shattering it at their feet. And he just walked away.

The memories of her bright smile melted away to the look of hurt and disappointment. Dean closed his eyes tight, trying not to see those images. He didn't mean to hurt her or lead her on. He enjoyed their time together, but they were always going to have to part. He was always going to have to come home to California.

Rubbing his head, he sat up. Opening his laptop, he dove into the world of distraction amidst countless emails and spreadsheets that demanded his attention. Dean did his best to absorb himself into his work, focus on work and escape the images, thoughts, and yearnings that were weighing heavy on his heart.

The moment Dean stepped into the office before he had a chance to lay his briefcase down at his desk, Marshall was bellowing for him to join him.

Dean paused, closing his eyes briefly. He collected himself. Pivoting, he complied and followed his boss' bellowing voice. Poking his head in the office, Marshall pointed toward a chair in front of him, "Have a seat."

Marshall sat with his elbows on the desk. His hands were

clasped together in front of him, touching his pursed lips. Heaving a deep breath, he eyed Dean carefully.

"So, what the hell happened out there? The assignment was supposed to be a simple smile and sign, then hop on the next flight home. Not only did that not happen, but you spent an entire additional week running around in circles jumping through hoops like a circus dog. Not exactly how I picture my number one negotiator operating. You're my closer. You let those country bumpkins play you," Marshall blew up at Dean.

Dean was careful to pause and measure his response. "They had particular needs and areas that required careful analysis. For both parties' sake."

Marshall did not look convinced. "We only needed their primary location and their business entity. No one cares about the fat that needs to be shed anyway. You needed to get them signed and done. That is what we sent you for."

"No, sit. Cape Fear Commericial did the right thing," Dean said calmly.

Dumbfounded, Marshall furrowed his brows, "What do you mean they did the right thing?"

"Our acquisition was not right for them. Not the way we drew it up, at least," Dean confessed.

"It doesn't matter whether it was right for them. It was right for our portfolio, for our investors. That's who we work for. Who *you* work for. Not them," Marshall levied. "It will serve you well not to forget that."

Dean looked away briefly.

"Ah, the heck with it. Let those fools in North Carolina run their ragged business into the ground. This was the best deal they were going to get. I just would have thought our crack broker would have gotten the job done and on our terms," Marshall fumed. He continued to eye Dean with an air of disdain and disappointment.

"I did my best, sir," Dean offered meekly.

"Did you?" Marshall questioned.

"What does *that* mean?"

"I just can't help thinking you let them get to you. You lost it. Playing on your old turf in front of your old fans got in your head. You know how to play the game. You know how the five-point strategy works. Find out their pain points. Twist them deep until you reveal they are at their breaking point. Make them think you are the *only* option that could possibly save them," Marshall preached. "Ink the damned deal."

"I know how that stupid sales technique works. Maybe it could have worked with Cape Fear Commercial, but you know what, I'm glad it didn't do it that way," Dean defended.

"What?" Marshall was beside himself.

"There's another business theory that I think it's about time we started to employ," Dean spat.

"Oh yeah, what's that?"

"Do the right thing, and the money will come," Dean stated. "Maybe it is time we build companies *up* instead of breaking them down. They can grow without flying in there with a machete and a wood chipper."

"Don't go getting all soft on me now. You are still our best man. You had a bad deal. Shake it off. Now move on. Your future as a principal is still there. You just stumbled a bit. You're going to have to make up some lost ground after this one."

"Maybe," Dean shrugged. "I've got to get back to work. I need to make up for lost time on the deals here in LA that I put on hold for the Carolina trip."

"The best thing to do. Just like dating, get back in there. Ink a deal or two and push forward. Get back in the game, Dean," Marshall suggested.

Standing up, Dean nodded without conviction. "I've got plenty to catch up on. I'll tackle the next on the docket."

"There you go, kid. Knock that one down, and then maybe we can relook at getting you on track for partner again. I'm not going to lie, though. Eyes are going to be all over you for a bit," Marshall warned Dean.

"Yes, sir," Dean acknowledged and left his boss' office.

Chapter Twenty-Three - California Dealing

Dean sat across the boardroom table from his client. He carefully outlined his review of the business' assets. "These three locations are in serious jeopardy. They have all struggled for multiple quarters. Not managing them back into viability prior to acquisition would be catastrophic for those sites and the employees."

The business owner studied the charts that Dean had laid out on the table. "These sites have been subpar facilities for a long time. We had them on the chopping block, but since their release wouldn't change our financials, we left them for you to do what you want with them," the owner said.

"I can build in some metrics and timetables for each site and fashion a turnaround for each location. I could at the very least, get them to break even value," Dean suggested. "If you like, I can put contingencies in the paperwork that requires Dana

Holdings to keeps them through that period. Give those sites and the people that work there a chance."

"What will that do to our deal?"

"I can get the paperwork done in a week. Your attorneys will probably want time to review the changes. I could have us back at the table in two weeks tops," Dean informed.

The man contemplated Dean's proposal. "Those sites have been a drag on our company for way too long. I am not willing to risk the deal for a few hundred workers who were piece-mealing together a subpar facility. No, let's sign this thing. Once we close the deal, I'll let you guys manage the pink slips or whatever it is you decide."

Dean sat for a moment studying the man.

"Is there something else? If not, I have folks waiting for me in my Dodger Stadium luxury box."

"No, I guess that's it. I don't need to keep you," Dean admitted, gathering the papers.

As Dean headed out of the office building, he watched an employee walk to her car ahead of them. Fumbling with her keys outside of a hobbled minivan, she cranked the ignition only to hear a stuttering, metallic sound for her effort.

The executive Dean had just signed papers with walked past the woman without any notice or recognition of her presence. The grinding noise from her car finally resulted in a start before choking and coughing to an abrupt halt.

The executive never glanced up, glibly entering his gleaming Mercedes. Firing his vehicle up, he put it in gear and sped away.

Dean walked up to the woman, knocking softly on her windshield to get her attention. Looking out of the driver's window, the woman hesitated at the stranger standing beside her van. Understanding that she needed help, she relented. Opening her door, she greeted him, her weary eyes looking at him with hope.

"Rosie, I'm Dean. Let's see what we've got going on here," Dean tried turning the ignition. The starter clattered to life, and the engine tried to turn over.

"The battery is good. The starter's probably at the end of its life, but it *is* working. I can hear the fuel pump motor," he said.

Rosie stared at Dean blankly as he ran through the modest diagnosis list that he knew. Snapping his fingers, he had an idea. Spying a wire hanger in her backseat, he asked for it and walked to the back of the van.

Opening the gas gap, he fed the hanger down the shaft as he straightened out lengths. Hitting bottom, he pulled it back out. First, visually inspecting and then smelling the length of the hanger, he asked, "Does your gas gauge work?"

The woman wrinkled her nose, "It sticks sometimes."

"When's the last time you filled up?"

"Sunday, but I only had enough for half a tank," Rosie

admitted.

"Okay. That's sort of good news, because if I'm right, it's an easy fix," Dean replied. "I think you are out of gas."

Rosie looked at Dean for a moment, unsure of what to do with the news. Dean felt he understood. Pulling forty dollars out of his wallet, he handed it to Rosie. She froze with the bills in front of her.

"It's okay," Dean assured. "I'm going to call my roadside service and get you a few gallons to get you going." Pulling out his phone, he opened the app and summoned the service.

Leaning against the van, he crossed his arms and smiled, "So, tell me about Kittridge Industries…"

Rosie shared that she typically worked at an alternate site but had been picking up additional shifts to catch up on bills. The extra travel likely impacted her gas budget as well, Dean presumed.

Dean asked her about the executives, explicitly calling out the man who drove away from his employee despite her clearly needing assistance. He learned that executives and employees rarely interacted with one another.

Looking at her carefully, Dean asked, "Which site do you normally work at?"

"Inland Empire," Rosie replied.

Dean watched the car service truck pull into the parking lot. "If I may give you advice, start looking for a different job."

Rosie looked up at him, questioning.

Dean knew he couldn't say more. That sentence alone would violate a handful of regulations and agreements. Rosie seemed to understand that Dean was there to meet with the company president. She nodded, suggesting she realized that he couldn't say more.

Once the car attendant put several gallons of gasoline into the minivan, he had Rosie start the vehicle up. It sputtered to life with a few groans but was otherwise running fine.

Dean thanked the attendant.

Turning to Rosie, he saw her eyes well up with appreciation.

"It looks like you're ready to go," Dean said. "Good luck, Rosie. It was nice to meet you."

"Thank you. You are very kind," Rosie said.

As she drove away, Dean slowly walked back to his car. He started thinking about the number of similar deals that he had put together for Dana Holdings. How many Rosies, had he personally put on the chopping block without reservation, without a moment's concern?

He celebrated owners, CEOs and boards wanting to close deals quickly, regardless of the cost of moving forward. Now, the thought of proceeding made him feel sick. Looking at the contract on his passenger seat, he felt like taking the folder and tossing it out of the passenger window, allowing the papers to rain down like snowfall on the California freeway.

His mood didn't improve as he laid on the brakes to avoid the sea of red taillights in front of him. The line of cars snaked their way for as far as he could see. With a sigh, he settled in for the long, slow drive home.

Flipping through his music options, he landed on one he usually skipped by. This time, selecting it, it felt strangely comforting and almost defiant in his current setting. Songs of dirt roads, beaches, and simpler lives filled his BMW's speakers for the first time. His L.A. rebellion lifted his spirits as he decided which of the eight lanes he wanted to drive down.

Dean arrived at his condo. Sticking his key into the lock, he looked down the hall toward his neighbors. One returning as he was, the other leaving. He realized he had no idea who they were. He hadn't introduced himself, nor had they. Dean paused to say hello to the neighbor, walking his way toward the stairs. The man never lifted his head and, in fact, made a circuitous step away from Dean's door as he approached.

Nodding to himself, Dean should have anticipated that response. Shrugging, he tossed his keys on the hall table and entered his sparsely furnished home. Pulling a beer from his refrigerator, he opened his patio doors and leaned against the railing.

On the streets, the boardwalk, and the beach beyond him,

he saw so many people buzzing about below him. In every direction, there were people. Yet, somehow, he felt very much alone.

Suddenly, Dean's phone buzzed, snapping him out of his thoughts. Looking at the screen, he saw Marshall's name and face pop up. Staring at it for a moment, Dean swiped the red Decline button and slid it back into his pocket.

Leaning over the railing, he stared out at the Pacific, feeling his emotions oscillate between numb and energetically defiant. He was hoping his contemplation, or maybe his beer, would determine the winner between the two.

Dean was hopeful that agreeing to meet Ray would pull him out of his funk and be the reset that he needed. Pulling up into the parking lot, he killed his music and grabbed the slip handed to him by the valet.

Finding Ray at an outside table, he gave a quick wave. Working his way through the crowd, he made his way to the table. Ray got up and gave his friend a half-handshake, half-man hug.

"How've you been? I haven't seen you since you got back" Ray exclaimed.

"My boss has been on me since not closing the Carolina deal. I've had a lot of makeup work to do," Dean admitted glumly.

"Dean Taylor failed to close a deal. Never thought I'd hear those words," Ray shook his head. "On a serious note, I'm deeply concerned about you, my friend. Did I hear country music coming from your car when you hit the valet? I thought you *hated* country music."

"I did…I do…I don't know. I think maybe I kind of like it?" Dean replied, unsure of the words seeping from his mouth.

Ray cocked his head and stared at his friend, awaiting further explanation.

"What? There's something wholesome and simple about it," Dean shrugged.

"All right," Ray nodded suspiciously. Suddenly his eyes grew wide, "A girl! It's about a girl!"

Dean looked hard at Ray for a moment. Suddenly his head was filled with visions of Shelby. "There's something to that."

"Old flame in North Carolina?" Ray asked, excitedly leaning into the conversation.

"No. Though I did run into plenty of those," Dean admitted. "We just kept running into each other. Turned into a simple dinner, turned into maybe a little more."

"And?" Ray pressed.

"And I had to come home," Dean shrugged.

Ray studied his friend for a moment, as though knowing there was more to the story. "Did something go wrong? You've met tons of girls that you only knew for a week."

"Nothing went wrong, except…I shouldn't…" Dean mumbled and looked away.

"Shouldn't? Shouldn't what?" Ray furrowed a brow.

Dean sighed, "I shouldn't have let it develop. She lost her husband...I knew I was leaving."

Ray nodded, "You let her get close, weren't exactly clear about your tenure, and left her in your rearview."

"Something like that," Dean said softly. "And her kids..."

Ray nearly spit out his drink, "She had kids? And you met them?"

"Well, yeah," Dean squirmed. "It kind of worked out that way."

Ray shook his head, "What alternate universe did you cross on the other side of the Mississippi?"

Dean shot his friend a look that declared he did not want to have that discussion.

"Man, we're all adults. She made a choice too. Sometimes you have to enjoy things for what they are and move on. That's okay. Life experiences. It'll be alright," Ray tried to cheer Dean up.

"Yeah," Dean nodded, clearly not convinced.

Ray shifted in his seat, feeling the air at the table becoming thick.

"So, what happened with the gig?" Ray asked, trying to take the conversation in a different direction. Dean was always crisp with discussions about work.

"I could have closed it, but it was a bad deal. So I killed it," Dean replied, taking a sip of his drink.

Ray's eyes went wide, "You killed it? No wonder the boss is all over you."

"This job. When you dig past the numbers, some people and families feel the impact of the decisions we make," Dean explained.

"That's your job, right? Negotiate the deal. It's up to the boards to decide whether it's good for them or not. You don't pick the winners and losers as long as Dana Holdings wins," Ray conferred.

Dean's mind bounced from Cape Fear Commercial to Rosie in the parking lot.

"I'm not sure I'm necessarily interested in helping Dana Holdings choose who wins any more," Dean admitted.

"Uh, life costs money. Dana Holdings wins, you get paid," Ray said. "Kind of how the world works."

Ray paused to take a drink as he studied his friend. "You need a good night out on the town. We'll meet some ladies…get your mind calibrated. Re-Californiated."

Dean's expression belied his disinterest in the suggestion.

"You're really serious about all this stuff," Ray straightened up.

"Like you said, sometimes you have to enjoy things for what they are and move on," Dean acknowledged.

Twenty-Four -
Back to Carolina, Again

D ean leaned against the frame of the window, watching the clouds streak past. Looking down on the patchwork squares of farmland, he wondered how often he had flown overhead and discounted them. Thinking about the people that worked to make those things happen, their hard work sending food across the country, he certainly had a new appreciation for them.

As he studied the landscape, he wondered what life was like in those small communities. He wondered how well people knew each other, if they rose to help each other in common need like the people in Wilmington had.

As the airplane touched down, Dean had a decidedly different feeling than his last trip. This time he wasn't burdened. He wasn't itching to turn around and fly out.

Stepping off the plane, he took in a big inhale, put on his

sunglasses to fend off the bright sun, and strode forward with his travel bag tossed over his shoulder. Generally, one to travel light, he nearly forgot to find the baggage carousel to collect his luggage.

Wheeling to the curb, he found the ride service he had arranged from the plane. Handing the driver the address, he sat back and watched the town move past his window and transition to beach traffic.

Pulling up to his stop, Dean hit the tip button on his app and looked up at the ten-story building. Pulling his bags, he entered the front door.

Hitting the elevator button to the top, he looked left and right to collect his bearings and followed the hallway toward the unit on his phone. Waving the photo on the phone to the electronic lock, he heard it disengage. Swinging the door open, he strode into the tidy condo. Much like the beach house he had rented, the beach beckoned the moment anyone entered.

Dropping his bags, he made an immediate beeline for the set of doors that separated him from the ocean. Flinging them open, he allowed the ocean breeze, crashing waves and seagull calls to create the ambiance that he so loved. Pulling a card from a basket, his realtor scribbled, "Welcome Home." He was most certainly, home.

Giving the condo that he had only seen in online photos and videos, a thorough once over, he nodded in approval. The apartment was a great room that flowed from foyer to kitchen to living room to beachfront patio in one glorious, open to the Atlantic, space.

Flanked on either side were bedrooms with their own balcony and ocean views.

Dean laughed to himself. He was beachfront with twice the space for half as much as his previous rent in California. Still, he knew getting a job would be a top priority, right after a few other items he had on his checklist.

Heading downstairs, he waited outside of the lobby doors. He didn't have long to wait before Thomas pulled up in the minivan. Dean studied it for a moment and hopped in with a grin.

"I've got to pick up the kids," Thomas admitted with a shrug.

"I'm not judging. It's just good to see you, my friend," Dean said.

Thomas cast him a look, "You sure about all of this?"

"I'm sure," Dean nodded. "Thanks for giving me a ride."

"No worries, I kind of wanted to see the whites of your eyes in person, anyways," Thomas grinned.

Dean chuckled, "Yeah, I probably would have to."

"Well, here we are," Thomas announced, pulling into a parking lot. "You want me to hang in case you don't find anything?"

"Nope, I'm good," Dean affirmed. "We still on for dinner, Friday?"

"We are. We're going to see you at church on Sunday, right?"

"You are," Dean nodded. With a pat on the roof of the minivan, he spun to tackle his task.

Looking upon a sea of vehicles lined up row after row, he waved off the salesman and strode directly toward his find.

Walking right up to the Jeep Wrangler, he gave it a once over, checked the odometer, and spun back to the salesman who was hustling to keep up. "Oh, that's a nice one. What kind of terms are you lookin' for?"

Staring at the man for several long moments, Dean pulled a wad of bills that he carried from selling his BMW. Rifling through the stack, he handed a portion to the salesman. "Here are my terms."

The man counted the bills and frowned, "Well, hold on, now. The price is on the window..."

"It is three grand more than you paid for it. I gave you one grand more, five hundred for you, five hundred for the dealership," Dean said.

The man studied the bills, still trying to decipher the arrangement.

"Can I have the keys?" Dean asked. "And the bill of sale. Not the twenty-page thing you guys put together, the back of the DMV registration version. Thanks."

Still frowning, the man scurried off, staring at his bills.

Dean had lowered the manual top on the Jeep and adjusted the seat and mirrors to his liking by the time the salesman and a man, Dean assumed to be his manager, came sauntering out.

"That's one fine machine," the man behind the salesman bellowed.

Dean turned and scowled at the man. Without words, the two men stared at each other for several full minutes before the man spoke, "I can see you are a man of great conviction. I tell you what..."

"I counted three Jeeps, roughly the same age as this one on the drive in. I'll admit, I like the color of this one *slightly* better. That's why I gave you a grand over your cost as opposed to making you two figure out how to split five hundred. How much you want to bet any one of those others will take the five?" Dean asked, still sitting in the driver's seat.

The man started to speak, looked at his salesman, and then back to Dean. "Alright, alright. Give him the keys. Here, this is the paper to take to the DMV. It's yours," the sales manager said.

Accepting the slip of paper, Dean looked at the salesman and then at the sales manager.

"Give him the keys," the manager nudged the salesman.

"Thanks, guys! Start doing business this way. I might start referring people to you," Dean said. Starting up the Jeep, he put it in gear. Looking over his shoulder, he backed out past the two salesmen and pulled away.

His next stop brought a smile to his face as the breeze streamed through the open-top Jeep. Pulling into the parking lot, he hopped out.

Entering the store, a clerk greeted him with a nod, and the sound of reggae music through the shop's speakers.

Walking with confidence, he strode up to a section of bamboo-clad boards pulling one out of the rack. He sized it up. Rubbing the bamboo surface, he grinned. With a hoist, he carried it up to the counter and dropped more of his BMW money.

Dropping the rear seats on the Jeep, he tucked the surfboard in and instinctively drove toward Crystal Pier. The surf tempted him to tackle the rolling waves before dark fell.

With a hop in his step, he bounded up the stairs. As customary, the doors opened, and two young ladies greeted him. Pulling off his sunglasses, he strained his neck toward the interior of the restaurant.

"Are you meeting someone?" the hostess asked.

Dean turned, his sunglasses in hand, "I was hoping to see Shelby…"

The hostess looked mildly surprised, giving Dean a wry glance over, she replied, "Shelby doesn't work here anymore. It looks like it's her loss…"

"Do you know where she went, I mean, works now?"

"I'm sorry," the hostess said. "I don't, and we wouldn't be able to say anyways. I'm sorry."

"That's okay," Dean nodded. Walking out to the parking lot, he put his sunglasses on. Searching the area, he chastised himself for doing so, knowing that he was not going to reveal her.

Checking his watch, he relented to returning to his condo. Climbing back into his Jeep, he pointed the steering wheel toward his new home. Pulling into the parking garage, he hoisted the surfboard over his shoulder.

Heading toward the elevator, he hesitated. Abruptly turning, he walked briskly toward the boardwalk to the beach right outside his condo. With a smile, he kicked off his shoes and jogged toward the waves. Tossing his board in ahead of him, he dove into the water with outstretched hands gripping the bamboo and pulling it under him.

He wasted no time reaching past the breakers and finding the swell line where he could observe the incoming sets. Finding an undulating grouping he liked, he dropped down and gave several quick strokes to get his momentum up and hopped on top of the board. Working the tail and nose, he coaxed as much from the soft roller as he could before bailing into the surf.

Looking up, he identified his condo, pleased that he lived a stone's throw from hitting the waves like he just had. Smoothing his ocean-soaked hair back, he spun his board and paddled out for another ride.

Twenty-Five -
The Search

As the morning sun shone its array of pinks, oranges, and yellow into his bedroom, Dean kicked his sheet off and sat up. He stared out at the ocean. The morning had brought a calm, glassy surf to the beach. There was such a peace to the entire scene.

Peace had largely filled Dean's heart, with a few notable exceptions. One of those exceptions, he had hoped to put ease that day. Climbing out of bed, he showered, foregoing the beach run that beckoned him.

In minutes, he was in the parking garage, firing up the Jeep. Pulling down Lumina Drive, Dean enjoyed the open-air morning. Parking the four-wheel drive, he hopped out. Flinging open the screen door, he perked the attention of the barista.

"Almond Milk!" Olivia exclaimed, a broad smile across her lips.

Dean frowned, "Really?"

"It's an identifier," Olivia shrugged cheerily.

"I suppose it is," Dean admitted.

"Your usual latte?"

"Yes, please," Dean nodded.

"I didn't think I'd see you again. You left right after the storm, right?" Olivia asked.

"I did."

"Well, it's good to see you, just the same," the barista sang from behind the espresso machine.

"It's nice to see you, too," Dean said. As he reached for his latte, he paused for a moment before taking the burden of grip away from Olivia, "Hey, do you know Shelby James?"

Olivia nodded, "She worked up at the pier restaurant."

"Yeah, that's her. You don't happen to know where I could find her?" Dean asked.

"I haven't seen her in weeks. Not long after the storm, actually," Olivia wrinkled her nose. Her eyes widened, "You like her!"

"I do," Dean said softly.

"Ya'll'd make a nice couple," Olivia said, approving.

"That was a lot of contractions, but thank you."

"Nice to have you back," Olivia called.

"Nice to be back," Dean raised his coffee cup as an affirmation.

Climbing into the Jeep, he picked up his cellphone. Dialing a number, he heard Allie's cheery voice. "Hi, Dean. We're looking forward to seeing you on Friday."

"I'm looking forward to seeing you all, too," Dean answered. "Hey, do you know where I can find Shelby?"

"Oh, Dean. I haven't seen her since the day after the storm. She and the kids haven't been at church, either."

"Hmm," Dean grunted, his mind drifting away.

"Have you tried the restaurant?"

"Yes, and the coffee shop. Same deal. No one has seen her since the clean-up," Dean said.

"I don't know what to tell you," Allie admitted.

"It's okay," Dean replied. "See you Friday."

Closing his eyes, both hands on the wheel, he tried to come up with an idea, but none came immediately to him. Site by site, he began retracing the steps that he had enjoyed with Shelby.

Starting with Airlie Gardens, he revisited the pier, the tree and the garden pavilion. Moving downtown, he walked along the riverfront. Symptoms of the storm were still evident, though the town had done a remarkable job cleaning up.

He circled the parking lot of the USS North Carolina Battleship. Shaking his head, he didn't know what he would expect to find other than memories. Those, he found aplenty.

Sighing, he put the Jeep in gear and pulled away. Hitting the highway, the wind and freedom of driving the Jeep lured him.

Losing himself in the sensation, finding a calm in the experience, he kept driving.

Finding himself at a junction, he turned and headed south. Driving until he reached the southern shore of Southport, Dean combed the town. In spite of himself, he drove to his old family home. He paused only a moment, noting the missing "For Sale" sign. With a smile toward the old place, he pushed on.

Completing the circuit, he drove to the confluence of the Cape Fear River and waiting in line for the ferry to Kure Beach. He couldn't help but inspect the cars pulling into the queue, slightly disappointed when each time it wasn't Shelby and the kids.

When the boat arrived, he followed the cars in his line and parked in tight formation on the bottom deck. Walking up the stairs to the top passenger level, he found a spot up front, leaning against the rail.

As the ferry's engine shifted into gear and the propellers started churning, Dean smiled at the slight hint of diesel that mixed with the salt mist. Pushing away from the landing, he watched as the ferry maneuvered into the channel. The big boat carved through the water and headed across the mouth of the Cape Fear.

Midway through the journey, the ferry's horn sounded briefly followed by the reply from the ferry heading southwest to the Southport Ferry Terminal. Passengers on either boat offered friendly waves to their cross bound counterparts.

Dean froze as his eyes lit upon one passenger. The moment was fleeting, and he couldn't be sure. Turning his head, he followed the ferry until it was out of sight. He stared at the water between the two distancing boats. Motionless, his mind tried to reconcile whether he was imagining what he wanted to see or if he had actually seen Shelby. Ultimately, he knew it didn't matter. By the time they docked, and he boarded a return ferry, she would be long gone, if it was her in the first place, which he knew it likely wasn't.

Hanging his head, he watched the bow of the boat cut a path to the Fort Fisher Ferry Terminal on Kure Beach. Reluctantly leaving the top deck, Dean climbed back into his Jeep and followed the taillights in front of him until he was back on land.

In his rearview mirror, he watched the slow pulsing flash of the Oak Island lighthouse. Shaking his thoughts, he scoffed at himself. He had to quit imagining her at every point of reference he had spent with her.

Pressing the Jeep forward, he pulled into his condo parking space. Not entirely feeling like going inside, he walked toward the beach. The evening sky was turning darker shades of blue, and the early moon glowed in its contrast.

Dean shuffled through the sand, casting his shoes aside near the condo's wooden walkway. Heading toward the firmer sand that had been tamped down by the action of the waves, he walked. Along the ocean, he couldn't classify his mood as anything but pleasant. He couldn't find Shelby. He wasn't sure what he was going to do for work, yet he was oddly content.

Walking past his former rental house and then past the Crystal Pier, he couldn't help but cast a gaze toward the restaurant, hoping for a glimpse of someone he knew wouldn't be there. Enjoying the night for what it was, he continued. He would watch families pack up from their final beach adventures of the day. He would catch couples arriving at the beach to enjoy evening walks hand in hand along the surf. He envied both.

Stopping, he stood for what seemed like hours just watching the waves roll in the moonlight. The Atlantic consoled him like a lifelong friend.

Dean spent the week with a subconscious eye on all the last known places where he had spent time with Shelby and the kids. He started his day on the beach. He ended his day on the beach. He visited Olivia each morning for a latte.

He had dinner with Allie, Thomas, and their kids on Friday, playing board games after their meal. He went to church on Sunday, craning his neck every time someone entered the sanctuary. Signing up to volunteer through a group at church, he began working and playing with children who didn't have a father figure in their lives.

At his condo, he made a concerted effort to get to know everyone on his floor and those he met in the lobby or heading upstairs.

Interviewing at a local marina, he took on contract work selling used boats and yachts. He even took the opportunity to recommend Cape Fear Commercial when he had the chance.

Every evening, he stood at his open bedroom patio door, reveling in the coastal breeze and sound of the waves chorusing against the sand. He would plop on his bed, fulfilled except for one Shelby-sized hole plaguing his thoughts as he closed his eyes and drifted away.

Twenty-Six -
The Offer

Dean woke as he usually did, opening a single weary eye. The call of the blue sky and beckoning surf urging him to come to life.

Climbing out of bed, he donned his swim shorts, plucked his board off of the wall, and headed for his morning session.

Tackling the moderate surf, he paddled his way back through the breakers and into the swells multiple times before returning to his condo to shower. Prepared to cycle through his day of coffee, churning through boat inquiries and meeting buyers for showings and signings, he was surprised when there was a knock at his door.

Towel slung over his shoulders, he walked to his foyer and pulled the door open. He was surprised to see Cassie standing there, smiling at him. She was clad in business wear, making him feel awkward in his wet swim trunks and a rolled towel over his bare chest.

"Hello?"

"Hi, Dean, I hope I'm not interrupting something," Cassie asked coyly.

Dean shook his head with a sheepish grin, "No, just heading into the shower. Morning swim. Then off to work."

"I see," Cassie said. "That's kind of what we wanted to talk to you about...work."

"We?" Dean frowned, peering over Cassie's shoulder.

A small entourage assembled behind her. Each individual made him feel even more self-conscious about his current state. As Bart Stevens strode through the group, he only succumbed more so.

Spinning around, he spied his laundry basket at the edge of the kitchen counter. In a few quick steps, he snatched a shirt from the pile and pulled it over his head, casting the towel aside.

By the time Mr. Stevens had arrived at his threshold, his shirt was in place. He was disheveled, but clothed.

"Mr. Stevens," Dean said, clearly surprised to see him at his condo doorway.

Mr. Stevens flashed a smile, "I heard you were back in town."

"I am," Dean nodded.

"I also heard from your boss."

"Former boss."

"Yes," Mr. Stevens nodded. "I heard that too. He went to a lot of trouble to convince me that accepting their deal as it was originally constructed way was the only way we could possibly survive as a company. He's pretty convincing, almost had me for a moment too. Actually told him I would think about it."

Dean grinned a sly grin, "Let me guess, dig up all of your pain points and declare how only Dana Holdings could swoop in and be your savior?"

"Something like that," Mr. Stevens admitted.

"One of the reasons I left," Dean said. "I hate that sales strategy."

Stevens nodded, "Then, when a little bird told me that you had returned, I had a different thought. I had another way that we could thrive as an organization, if you will."

"Oh?" Dean eyed the CEO.

"I thought, how about I hire *you* to run Cape Fear Commercial's business development and contract negotiations? I may not be able to one hundred percent retire as I hoped, at least not right away. But I think with you in charge of running our deals. I could feel pretty good about slipping away a bit more. What do you say?" Mr. Stevens looked at Dean, hopefully.

"Are you serious?" Dean's eyes widened.

"You have the business acumen. That was never in question," Mr. Stevens shared. "You have proven that you have the right moral fiber, suggesting you are done running away from your problems."

"I wish everyone felt the same," Dean mumbled softly.

Mr. Stevens cocked his head, "What?"

Shaking his head, Dean said, "Nothing…I, uh, I accept. I accept!"

"Great!" Mr. Stevens held out both of his hands to clamp down on Dean's in a hearty shake.

"When would you like me to start?" Dean asked.

"Get yourself acclimated. I hear you have a job if you need to give notice."

Dean shrugged, "Just a little contract work. No worries."

"I'll let you work out the details with Cassie. We'll find you a spot in the downtown office in the meantime," Mr. Stevens said.

"Thank you, Mr. Stevens."

The CEO squared up to Dean. "I'm genuinely glad to have you aboard, Dean. Tell you what, unless you've got plans, join my wife and me this weekend. I'll send you the details."

"It'd be my pleasure," Dean nodded.

Mr. Stevens turned and walked down the hall, Jacob and Chester followed.

Cassie rocked back on her heels, a wide grin across her face. "Welcome aboard."

"When I came here…when I saw who I was going to be working with, I never would have figured things would have turned out this way," Dean admitted.

"Who knew you were all grown up," Cassie teased.

Dean scowled, "Mostly."

Cassie cocked her head, studying him carefully. "The girl? Got close to her. Worse, you let her get close to you...and you left."

"That's about the size of it," Dan admitted sullenly.

"Well, you're back *now*," Cassie noted, hopefully. "Looks like you're putting down roots." Cassie scanned his condo.

"A little too late. She's gone," Dean said.

Cassie frowned, "Gone?"

Shrugging, Dean said, "No one knows. Not at the restaurant. Hasn't visited her coffee shop. Hasn't gone to church."

"Hmm. Well, that *is* something," Cassie mused. With a suspicious look, she asked, "Is that why you came back? For her?"

"That was a factor. I like spending time with Shelby and her kids," Dean admitted. "But it was more than that. Coming back reminded me, or maybe struck for the first time, what this place and the people here mean to me."

Cassie grinned, "Wow, that sounded like a Hallmark card."

Rolling his eyes, Dean said, "It's true."

"I'm glad," Cassie rested her hand on his arm. "It's good to have you back."

"Thank you," Dean said.

"I'll send you some stuff to review to get you ready. Nothing pressing, just let me know when you are ready to start,"

Cassie said.

"I will," Dean nodded.

As she walked away, he closed the door and leaned against it. Staring down the hallway toward the Atlantic skyline framed by his patio doors, he thought how fortunate he was that Mr. Stevens tracked him down. He wasn't sure what the man saw in him, but he was glad to have his confidence.

Twenty-Seven - Carolina Beach Life

Dean spent the week following Mr. Stevens' surprise visit getting his new life in order, at least in between making use of good surf reports. He found the change of pace away from his frenetic California lifestyle allowed him to enjoy people more. Instead of merely grabbing his coffee and running out, he stayed to visit with Olivia. He began to know the regular visitors to the coffee shop. He made it a tradition to buy someone else coffee, targeting veterans when he could.

Devouring the materials that Cassie sent over, he met her midweek to set his starting timeline the following Monday. Part of his role would be to ensure that anyone coming to Cape Fear Commercial negotiated reasonably, and he could exercise his experience to ensure the people and legacy would remain intact.

Dean snuck time in to sell a couple of boats in between work prep and surf sessions.

By the time the weekend rolled around, he was driving toward Figure Eight Island, where Mr. Stevens and his wife lived. Pulling into their drive, he found the setting an oddly pleasant mix of charming yet elegant.

The large home had a grand entrance with an expansive wrap-around Mediterranean porch leading to the protected waters of the inlet. Despite the opulence, he was met by two very down to earth hosts. Mr. Stevens and his wife greeted Dean as he climbed the steps to the ornate wooden double doors of the house.

"We're so glad you could make it," Mrs. Stevens said.

"It's my pleasure," Dean said. "You have a beautiful home."

"You can be our guest anytime," the Stevens matriarch said.

"Careful what you offer," Dean grinned.

"Honey, why don't you take Dean out to the patio? I'll bring a tray of goodies for you to nibble on," Mrs. Stevens suggested.

Nodding, Mr. Stevens led Dean toward the rear of the house. "Cassie says you're going to start Monday."

"Yes, sir," Dean nodded.

Mr. Stevens paused at the bank of French doors lining the entire living room. Hand on the doorknob, he shot Dean a stern look, "In my home, it's just Bart. No, Mr. Stevens, no sir- unless you're one of my kids, that is."

"Your house, your rules," Dean beamed.

"Let's get you properly situated. Cocktail?" Mr. Stevens

offered.

"That'd be great. Whatever you're having," Dean agreed.

Mr. Stevens sauntered to his outdoor bar set up near a massive grill and pizza oven.

Walking toward the rail overlooking the water, Dean found familiar faces in chaise lounges overlooking the inlet.

"Hi guys," he announced himself.

Cassie and Chester turned their heads, "Hi Dean!"

Chester stood up. His linen pants and silk shirt suited the lovely patio experience properly. Extending a hand, he exclaimed, "Good to see you, Dean."

"Nice to see you as well, Chester."

"Welcome aboard," Chester shook his hand heartily.

Dean looked slightly put off, Chester had not shown him much notice throughout their encounters. "Thank you."

"I'll admit, I wasn't sure about you when you first showed up. I didn't like the idea of Pops selling the company. I really didn't like the idea of the business going to some slick California outfit. You showed that you cared. You're a stand-up guy," Chester confessed.

"People and legacy are important," Dean admitted. "I'm glad he didn't sell. We have some work to do ahead of us, but we'll get there. The Stevens family will own Cape Fear Commercial for a long time to come."

"Woah, woah, woah," Mr. Stevens bellowed as he

approached, holding two cocktails in front of him, gesturing his protest. "No shop talk on the patio after five o'clock on Friday!"

All heads turned toward the patriarch and Cape Fear Commercial CEO.

"Sorry, Dad," Chester proclaimed sheepishly.

"I like the rule," Dean acknowledged.

"Oh, sure. Suck up to the boss," Cassie ribbed him.

Handing Dean a cocktail, he urged him toward the patio chairs. "Sit. Take a load off. Comfort and tranquility is why I bought the place," Mr. Stevens shared.

"You bought the place because Mom liked it," Chester scoffed.

"Well, sure, there was that," Mr. Stevens confessed.

Eyeing the dock that led notably far out into the inlet, Dean asked, "May I?"

"Of course," Mr. Stevens nodded. "I'll join you."

Heading toward the dock, they strolled, drink glasses in hand.

"Once in a while, you'll see dolphins playing here," Mr. Stevens informed him.

"That's a bonus," Dean said. "This is… this is wonderful."

"Thank you. Took a lot of hard work to get her," Mr. Stevens admitted.

Dean scanned the water, "I know. Well, deserved."

Mr. Stevens leaned against the rail as they reached the end

of the long, wooden dock. He sipped his cocktail before addressing Dean pointedly, "Seen Shelby, since you've been back?"

Dean dropped his head, "No, sir."

"Bart."

"Right, Bart," Dean nodded. "It's not for lack of trying. She seems to have left town not long after I did."

"Oh? Have you called her?"

Dean laughed, "Yes. A few times. She hasn't answered my calls."

Mr. Stevens closed his eyes. "I see. I'm sorry to hear that. You two seemed…really good together."

"I was beginning to think so," Dean admitted.

Looking out at the soft current of the protected waterway, Mr. Stevens leaned back and sighed. "People need to process things. When we have expectations and life doesn't meet them, sometimes we need to gather ourselves. Come back, refreshed."

"Or we abandon them because we started to see the negative expectations we feared in the first place," Dean countered.

"Is that what you think happened?"

"I do."

Mr. Stevens stared off thoughtfully. "Sometimes you get one chance and that chance shapes you. You get to use that experience for something…or someone else down the road, if you learn from it. Other times, you never know when that second chance may present itself."

"Sure," Dean nodded half-heartedly. His eyes centered on an egret launching itself from the shallows and gliding along the calm evening water.

The sound of footsteps against the wood decking of the dock gathered their attention. Cassie strode with a mission in their direction.

"Boys, I've been told to summon you for dinner," Cassie declared.

Mr. Stevens looked visibly disturbed, "Goodness, I was supposed to be helping!" Hustling down the dock, the patriarch jogged toward the house.

Cassie let out a giggle.

"What?" Dean asked, suspicious of her jovial outburst.

"So, so many things," Cassie grinned. "Seeing him hustle like he got stung by a bee for fear of Veronica's wraith. Seeing you mope around like a lost puppy…"

"Really? I'm good. I feel…very content," Dean scoffed.

Cassie looked at him with a raised brow.

"I am," he offered a nonchalant shrug as they headed toward the house.

"He likes you, Bart does," Cassie said.

"He's a good man," Dean replied.

Cassie nodded, "He is." Slipping her arm in his, she whispered, "Here's a little secret, so are you."

Twenty-Eight -
The (Not So) New Guy

D
ean started his role with Cape Fear Commercial unlike any other new job. He spent his first week completing the circuit that Cassie had taken him on. He spent an entire day at each facility meeting in-depth with heads of every department, from plant management to the janitorial staff.

He paused and introduced himself to everyone he walked past. At lunch, he found the busiest table to wedge himself into.

When he arrived at North Side, he was surprised when everyone stopped their duties and turned toward him. All at once, they broke into a standing ovation. With a hand in the air, he warmly thanked them. He shook as many of their hands as he could, reintroducing himself and listening to their names, trying to divine some method of remembering them all.

Dean studied the plant, taking in all of the people so

excited to have their jobs, to support their families. He was grateful that Mr. Stevens had Cassie work with him before signing. He was pretty sure the atmosphere would have a different tone, otherwise. His life would have, for that, he was sure.

Leaving the plant facility, he walked the path along the creek. Following it until the town came in to view, he paused. Studying the tiny main street, what it lacked in volume, it made up for in charm and polish.

He imagined the town without Cape Fear Commercial. There wouldn't be much, if anything left, he surmised. Completing the trail that dumped into the tiny village, Dean found his way to the little bakeshop.

"Hello there, Dean," the jovial Jan Evers called the moment he entered the shop when the bell atop the front door declared his presence. She watched the door expecting someone in his wake.

"Just me today," Dean admitted.

Jan rushed over, "It's good to see you. How is your first week at Cape Fear?"

Dean grinned, "News travels, huh?"

"In a small town," Jan sang. "What can I get you, hon?"

"Cup of coffee for sure. Why don't you surprise me with a pastry... Ooh, wait! Do you have apple fritters?" Dean asked.

"Just coming into season, I sure do," Jan nodded.

"Great," Dean smiled. "My first week is good. I am just spending time with the people. Mr. Stevens has taught me that is everything. All else takes shape from there."

"Smart man, that Mr. Stevens," Jan exclaimed.

"He is. I am blessed to be able to work with him," Dean admitted. "I'll learn a lot from him."

Jan placed a coffee mug and fritter in front of him. "Not everyone in your shoes is so eager to learn."

"Used to think I knew it all until I was proven to be wrong. Very wrong," Dean confessed.

Jan studied him for a second and smiled, "When Cassie brought you in, I thought you were a slick charmer."

"And now?"

"Charming, yes. Slick…not so much," Jan said.

"I'll take that as a compliment," Dean said.

"Do."

"How much?" Dean asked.

"On the house," Jan stated.

Dean shook his head and protested, "You can't do that all the time."

"House rules," Jan shrugged. "Keep taking care of the people at Cape Fear and the people of North Side, and it'll be on the house."

Dean looked thoughtful for a moment. Suddenly, a grin surfaced, "Alright. On a completely separate topic, I would like to order thirty dozen variety donuts every other Friday. Do you deliver?"

Jan eyes Dean with pursed lips. "You are slick, but well played."

With an approving smile, she added, "Welcome back to North Carolina and welcome to Cape Fear Commercial, hon."

Giving Jan his credit card information for the standing order, he thanked her and stepped back on to the quiet streets of North Side.

Heading back toward the plant, he had the solid resolve that there was a place to work, and the town remained solvent. He would do what he could to ensure it would stay that way. For the first time in his life, he felt not just successful, but good about what he was doing.

As the first week turned to the second, Dean began working on the guaranteed "no-fuss fit" canvas line from Cape Fear Commercial products. Working with Cassie, they created an entire marketing campaign and relaunch for every product that came from the North Side facility.

By the end of the campaign's first week, Dean had landed a national deal for the canvas line married to Cape Fear Commercial's traditional suite of products. The deal not only served to make strides in ensuring the viability of North Side but also its enduring success.

Twenty-Nine -
The Meeting

Dean heard the door to the office open. Glancing at the clock, fifteen minutes past the hour, he smiled, knowing that Mr. Stevens had arrived. Heavy footsteps up the stairwell toward Dean's second-floor office overlooking Oleander Drive affirmed that fact.

"Good morning, Dean," Bart's voice boomed as he reached the top of the stairs. "Boy, I've got to tell you, I am sure glad my office is on the first floor."

Dean laughed, "I kind of like it up here."

"Tell me that next August," Mr. Stevens beamed. "I know you have only been at it for a couple of weeks. I need you to go on a mission for me."

"Sure, whatever you need."

"I need you to go to Southport. Take the ferry across and head on to Oak Island. There is a marina there that does a surprising volume of yacht work," Mr. Stevens said.

"Okay. What's the situation?" Dean asked.

"They've been a long-time client for us. They're looking at switching to a Chinese vendor. I need you to negotiate a scenario that keeps them a customer yet keeps us profitable," Mr. Stevens said.

"No problem, I'll leave right away," Dean assured his boss.

"Great, I'll have Charlotte get you the address."

"I'll be right down," Dean said, gathering what he needed for the meeting.

Descending the stairs, he smiled at Charlotte, who was waiting for him. Handing him a sticky note with an address scribbled on it, she said, "Nice flowers."

"Asiatic lilies," Dean said. "Perfect for fall, don't you think?"

"Where'd you get them?" Charlotte asked.

"Garden near the back parking lot," Dean quipped.

Charlotte rolled her eyes, "You're just like Mr. Stevens. Can never get a straight answer from you, scallywags."

Dean grinned as he opened the front door, "Julia's Flower Shop."

Letting the door shut, Dean headed for his Jeep. The September weather was more than pleasant. The oppressive heat of August had passed, but the warm coastal air clung to a touch of summer.

Leaving the top down on his Jeep, he slid his sunglasses on and shifted into gear heading for the ferry to take him to Brunswick County and his meeting with the marina. With most of the tourists gone for the season, the drive through the beach towns of Carolina and Kure Beach held a different charm than the active summertime bustle of tourist season.

The pace took on a leisurely one as the year-long residents of the beach houses embraced coastal living with the tranquility of the sea. Dean studied the homes along the route, most clad in soft pastels with white porches and nothing but a stretch of sand and seagrass between them and the Atlantic.

Finding himself at the ferry terminal, he pulled to the front of the queue as a few hundred yards into the Cape Fear. He watched the scheduled boat pull away. Reclining his seat, he settled in to wait for the next boat to arrive.

Soaking in the sun, he closed his eyes. His visualization of the impending meeting soon drifted to the sleepy beach towns— the stark contrast between their lifestyles versus what he had in California.

It wasn't long before the sound of the ferry's horn broke his thoughts. Sitting up in his seat, he watched the cars stream off one by one before the attendant waved him aboard. Dean guided the Jeep into position and headed to the passenger deck.

Following the outer railing to a spot on the ocean side of the bow, Dean leaned with his forearms against the rail. Settling to enjoy the ride, he watched the churn of the Cape Fear water as the screws of the ferry displaced it as the big diesel engines chugged to life and pulled away from the dock.

Curving away from Fort Fisher and across the mouth of the river meeting with the saltwater of the Atlantic Ocean, the ferry chugged to speed toward the little town of Southport.

Dean laughed to himself. His commute to this meeting couldn't be more different than the stressful bumper to bumper battles he was used to Southern California or any city he traveled. With a deep breath, he decided that he could get used to it.

Letting his mind absorb the experience of being on the water, he was lulled into a blissful state watching the waves roll by. The voice behind him startled him, for many reasons.

"Hey, that's my spot," the voice declared.

Dean opened his eyes and slowly turned from the rail.

Shelby stood on the deck, staring at him. The breeze from the open water ferry softly, swaying strands of her hair across her face. Her summer dress flowed gently as the two looked at each other for several long moments before either found words.

"I heard you were back in town," Shelby said coyly.

"I am," Dean admitted. His ordinarily cool composure was completely hijacked by the beautiful woman before him, her hand tightly wrapped around his heartstrings.

"I heard you were doing some good things over at Cape Fear," Shelby continued.

Dean shrugged, "I hope so."

Shelby stared at him. Her arms crossed. "So, you're really back."

Nodding Dean answered, "I am, yes."

Biting her lip, Shelby seemed to assess him and how she wanted to respond. "What brought you back?"

"Something was tugging at me, that seemed to tell me this is where I was supposed to be. Where I belong," Dean shared.

"It's called roots," Shelby quipped.

Chuckling, Dean admitted, "Yeah, I've heard of such things."

"I was pissed at you," Shelby declared, her arms still crossed, though she had taken a step closer to him.

"I know," Dean conceded, his eyes dropping to his feet.

Stepping closer so that she was directly in front of him, looking him square in his eyes, she snapped, "You convinced me that you were safe. That I could open up to you, when I really, really didn't want to share my life with anyone. I let my guard down. I let you near my children."

Her eyes burned into his.

"You knew the whole time that you were leaving," Shelby spat.

Dean lowered his head. "I know. I didn't expect anything between us either. I just really enjoyed spending time with you...and the kids."

Shelby stared at him as though she were reading words from his expressions.

"When the time came, I didn't want to leave," Dean admitted softly.

"It's as much my fault. It's not like I didn't know you would be leaving. I believed for a moment what I wanted to believe, despite what I knew to be the truth. A part of me hung on your leaving as an excuse. An excuse to get close. An excuse to be mad when you left," Shelby admitted. Pressing curtly, she asked, "Tell me this. Are you done running?"

"I don't want to run. Not anymore." Dean stared out at the crashing waves.

Shelby nodded at his response; her expression was not yielding any insight into her thoughts or feelings.

"Where have you been? I tried to find you," Dean asked.

"I heard," Shelby admitted. "I went home to Mount Olive for a while. I needed to sort through things. I realized I needed to put a part of me…and the kids to a proper, peaceful rest."

Shelby swallowed hard, casting a glance out at the Atlantic's horizon before she continued.

"Allie called me a couple of weeks ago. I told her not to tell you that we spoke. I didn't know what I wanted to do, or where I was going to end up. I didn't know if I wanted to speak with you. I wanted to know you were going to be here to stay before I…before I saw you. Even then, I wasn't sure if I was going to speak to you,"

Shelby said. "I kind of watched you for a bit."

"Hidden in the corner, like at the coffee shop," Dean offered a faint smile.

"Maybe," Shelby shrugged, not a hint of humor in her voice. "Allie said you've been going to church."

"I have."

"That's good."

"It is," Dean admitted.

"She tells me that you bought a house," Shelby pressed.

"I did," Dean nodded and then shrugged. "Well, condo."

Shelby eyed him carefully, as if trying to locate something, "That sounds kind of permanent."

"I certainly hope so," Dean said. He looked intently into Shelby's eyes.

Shelby reached up with a hand on either shoulder and spun him to face her directly. Staring into his eyes, she arched her back to push her head forward until her lips were hovering inches from his. Pressing forward, her hands laced behind his neck, she kissed him intently.

"Welcome home, Dean Taylor."

About the Author

Seth Sjostrom is a serial entrepreneur, adventurer and author. His novels include the thrillers *Blood in the Snow, Blood in the Water, Blood in the Sand, Penance, Penance: Unredeemable, Penance: Absolution, Patriot X, Patriot X: Insurrection, Dark Chase and Dark Chase: Dead Run* as well as the romances *Back to Carolina, Finding Christmas, The Tree Farm, Letters from Santa, The Nativity* and *The Toy Store*. He recently released the first of his Beach House Mysteries series *Trouble on Treasure Island*. Seth partners with Hire Heroes USA with proceeds and volunteer hours dedicated with sales of his Patriot X series. Sales of *The Christmas Café* help to support Jen Lilley and Ale Boggiano's "Christmas is Not Cancelled" charity fundraising for foster children. Seth has also shares a portion of author proceeds of his Penance Series with the Mel Greene Institute to Stop Human Trafficking.

www.SethSjostrom.com
Twitter: @SethSjostrom
Facebook: @authorSethSjostrom
Instagram: @SethSjostrom

More Books by Seth

Christmas Titles
Finding Christmas
The Tree Farm
The Nativity
The Toy Store
The Christmas Café
Love at The Christmas Con

Beach House Mysteries
Trouble on Treasure Island
A Caper on Carolina Beach (2024)
Peril on Palm Beach (2025)

Other Titles
Back to Carolina
Penance
Penance: Unredeemable
Penance: Absolution
Dark Chase
Dark Chase: Dead Run
Patriot X
Patriot X: Insurrection
Blood in the Snow
Blood in the Water
Blood in the Sand

Children's Books
Letters from Santa
The Hollow
Cryptid Rangers: The Secret of the Skunk Ape
The Heart of a Reindeer (2024)
The(Too) Helpful Little Angel (2024)
A Puppy Whisperer Christmas (2024)

Printed in the USA
CPSIA information can be obtained
at www.ICGtesting.com
LVHW040859060624
782475LV00003B/160